Margaret's desire to write began at a young age, writing stories from her imagination. In between raising a family, Margaret Franceschini also devoted time in writing poems which were published in various local books and on poetry sites. She managed to continue her education at the local college, then began working with children with Autism.

One summer while vacationing with her family and watching children running through the sand, she remembered her summer vacations as a child with her family and a little boy who would look for her each weekend. This simple act of playing in the sand, digging with seashells and the memory of him running with her to the shore and back to the sand gave her the idea and title of her novel, *Seashells*.

In Remembrance:

A man of integrity who displayed his love and trust to all friends. He was a man of honor in all his actions, fair and worthy of respect. There was an unspoken commitment to his friends as well as top priority to his family. He gave me encouragement and hope as he supported me in all my writings and cheered me on to reach my goal. Forever in my heart, there will never be another, Andy Mele.

Margaret Franceschini

SEASHELLS

AUSTIN MACAULEY PUBLISHERS™

LONDON • CAMBRIDGE • NEW YORK • SHARJAH

Ordering Information
Quantity sales: Special discounts are available on quantity purchases by corporations, associations, and others. For details, contact the publisher at the address below.

Publisher's Cataloging-in-Publication data
Franceschini, Margaret
Seashells

ISBN 9781685621582 (Paperback)
ISBN 9781685621605 (ePub e-book)
ISBN 9781685621599 (Audiobook)

Library of Congress Control Number: 2023901104

www.austinmacauley.com/us

First Published 2023
Austin Macauley Publishers LLC
40 Wall Street,33rd Floor, Suite 3302
New York, NY 10005
USA

mail-usa@austinmacauley.com
+1 (646) 5125767

Table of Content

The deep current of the ocean carries a pearl essence, its grooves covered in swirls of blue as it dances on the rhythm of the waves. After floating through a long voyage, it finally rolls from the sea-foam to settle upon the warm, wet, yellow sand. At last, the tiny mollusk outgrew his home. In his wake, a magical imprint remains, for the now empty shell will bring the enchantment of love to the small hands that find it.

Chapter 1
Sunshine and Friendship

Parasols of every color in the rainbow filled the burning sand while laughter traveled through the air like a drumbeat, filling the atmosphere with the sounds of family fun.

They had just met at Holgate beach New Jersey on a hot summer day in July when their parents had laid out the beach blankets and set up the umbrellas. Their eyes met, and with a delighted nod to find each other, they began to play, running through the sand with a beach ball, throwing it over the volleyball net. As their pace became faster, her long legs floated in the air, showing the stamina from her training as a ballet dancer. They ran to the ocean and dipped their toes into the cold water; they were thrilled, but afraid to go too deep, for the waves were over their heads. Instead, they braced themselves for the surge of waves that rolled in and crashed against their little bodies. Then they shrieked, giggled, and joined hands to run back to the safety of the dry sand. Their friendship deepened as they played for a week in the sun and sand, never thinking it would ever end.

Playing the roles of royalty, he was her king and she became his queen as they pushed the sand into mounds, created deep channels around their castle, and waited for the ocean waves to fill their moat, then watched the water run into their castle and wash it all away.

In the glare of the sun and the expanse of the ocean, they felt safe holding on to each other's hands. The sand was warm and comforting under their feet as they ran to the shore and back, collecting seashells and filling their beach buckets to the top.

The boy's foot felt a smooth bump. He pushed away a layer of sand, and his coffee-colored eyes caught a gleam coming from an unusual shell.

"This is better than the sandbox," she said, arms spread wide and her emerald eyes twinkling.

"Sandboxes are for babies. I'm ten." He held the seashell up to examine his find. "I can't open this!" he exclaimed, comically imitating her gestures and holding up the large clam seashell.

His thick, dark eyebrows arched as he searched for an opening. Together, they tried using some pieces of driftwood. Finally, they found one long, thin stick that came to a point.

"Ah, maybe there's a pearl inside." She laughed the way a ten-year-old would laugh, with genuine excitement.

"If there is, I'll give it to you," he replied with a little sheepishness, blushing.

"I wonder what kind of creature lived in this," she said, running her little fingers along the spiral from the tip to base. Her eyes watched his slender fingers as he carefully pried open the shell with the sharp edge of the driftwood stick like a surgeon. She thought, *He has the fingers of a piano player.*

He gently handed her one piece of the shell. "It's empty! After all that work trying to get it open."

"Oh, it's okay. Look at the colors! They're blue and pink! It smells like the ocean," she said as she held it up. Her eyes sparkled with wonder at something so beautiful as the sun caught the shiny hues of red in her hair.

"I'll keep this piece, and you keep the other. Then tomorrow, we can bring them back here and use them for one of our castles." He spoke eagerly as a smirk played at the corner of his lip at the sight of his new friend.

"That's a great idea. I can't wait. This is our spot. We have to meet right here tomorrow, same time." Her eyes became set on his.

"My name is Cove. What's yours?"

"Heather. Mom says it's a flower."

"I don't know what mine means. It's just Cove."

They didn't speak but steadily gazed deeper and deeper into each other's eyes, and for a moment, no words were spoken. They smiled, and as they slowly connected their halves of the shell, a sort of brightness shone around them. Something beautiful kindled within them.

The memory became like a warm breeze to them when they recalled playing on a hot summer day and sharing a treasured shell that united their souls.

***

The next morning was warm but sunless as the gray sky fell into a misty fog. Silhouettes of families set up their cabanas in opposition to the vast blanket of mist that hung over the sand.

Cove's mother, Mary, couldn't help but notice other families carrying their blankets and coolers as they left their cottages for the beach as she regretfully heaved another suitcase into the car. She gave her neighbor a wave but wished she could stay another week. Then she went back into their cottage looking for her son.

"Cove, come on. Hurry up and help us pack the car. It's time to leave." She rolled her eyes in exasperation with a flushed face.

"But, Mom, I promised Heather I would meet her back at the beach today. I have the other half of the shell." His eyes became wide from the surprise that they were leaving, then with a single robotic motion he reached for the door.

"I'm sorry, son, but we have to leave; it's already been a week. Dad and I have work tomorrow. I have to get back to the hospital. I'm the chief nurse, and my staff is waiting for me. Now that I think of it, I have to train a few new nurses. And your father has some summer tutoring that he has to get done with his students before they leave for their vacations, so please, let's get going." She kept packing and moving clothes around like an investigator as she talked, trying to arrange everything in the luggage.

Cove pretended he was looking for his luggage. To him, her talking was all empty chatter, as he had something else on his mind.

"But, Mom, please, I know I can't wait any longer. Just let me run over there really quick. I just want to tell her the number of our cottage so she knows when we come back to look for me here."

"Cove, calm down, it's okay. We'll return for a couple of more weeks before the summer is over; don't worry. Just get your luggage."

Mary was tall and slender, with her long, soft, brown hair flowing down past her shoulders. Her eyes matched the coffee color of her son's. She was proud that they shared the same facial features. As she brushed aside her hair, Mary noticed again that her long, slender fingers were identical to his. As the chief nurse at the hospital, she was an effective leader, having the ability to handle stress and always offering advice on the best ways to improve facility care. Pointing in the direction of his luggage, she commanded him as if ordering a battalion.

Cove lowered his head and thought about it. Then, without anyone noticing, he tiptoed across the polished wood floors and ran out the back door. He knew his way around this town well because they always rented the same cottage each summer for weeks at a time. The beach was only two blocks away. It wouldn't take a long time to find her and tell her that he was leaving but would be back before the summer was over and to remember their meeting place and the shells.

He raised his hand against the heavy mist as he searched for his little friend. He ran in and out of families already setting up to spend the day on the beach, even though gray clouds concealed the sun. She wasn't in the spot where they had met yesterday. She wasn't anywhere. There was a new feeling in his stomach, something he never felt before as a crushing weight fell on his chest.

It must have been almost an hour later when he just dragged his feet back to their rental cottage with his half of the shell still in his hand.

His father, Joseph, threw up his hands in anger. "Where have you been, young man?" His eyes pierced through Cove's with his question.

Cove wasn't used to his father reacting out of fear because his personality was always humorous, and he had a calm demeanor. He hoped to not only resemble him with his thick, dark-brown hair and eyebrows, but to also inherit his calmness that gave him the ability to control a classroom. He wondered if he would become a teacher like his father.

Cove's father watched how his son became somber. As he looked at Cove, he realized his son could be as tall as his parents. He had always hoped his son would follow in his teaching profession. He like the idea that Cove had inherited his mother's long, narrow fingers. He remembered when Cove was younger how he would watch his son's eye-hand coordination. He was amazed at how Cove would explore his world with such advanced dexterity. *Maybe he will play the piano and be a part of the beauty of the orchestra. I can see his fingers moving across the pure ivory keys.* He sighed.

"I'm sorry, Dad. I was looking for Heather," Cove replied as sadness covered his face. Cove's father softened as his eyes searched his son's, and he regained his calmness.

"I have an idea. Let's pack up the car and take a ride to where we had set up our blankets. Maybe by then, she'll be there. And don't forget, we'll be back at this rental in three weeks. This is our summer home. And I bet her family comes here for their summer vacation as well."

At a leisurely pace, Cove's father drove the car around the block and passed the entrance of the beach, but she wasn't there.

Cove looked up from the back seat, his eyes pleading for understanding in the rearview mirror.

"Don't worry, Cove. We'll return before the summer is over. I believe she'll be here again like most families; this beach has become a tradition for a lot of them." His father said with a return look of understanding and words of comfort for his son.

They steadily drove on past the exit. Cove held his half of the shell while he kept looking out through the back window. As the horizon of the beach grew smaller, his eyes became tired, and he began to feel a nervous energy. He hoped he would return to the same place on the beach to find his new friend and match the other half of the shell.

***

That same morning, a mist covered the windows of the little white rental cottage where Heather was staying. Her mother, Margaret, had been packing her clothes into a suitcase and arranging Heather's in her luggage when she heard soft footsteps in the front room. Heather inched forward to the front door and was about to run out when her mother's voice rang in her ears.

"Heather, where do you think you are going?"

Margaret's voice was strong as her hands, which firmly gripped her hips. Her emerald eyes gave a long stare at Heather as she flicked back her long, red hair from her forehead. Not only had Heather inherited her mother's looks, she had also received her strong personality. This disposition was what helped Margaret to own two successful businesses with her husband, Richard.

Heather stood firm with her hands on her hips in defiance and imitation of her mother. "I'm just running out to the beach to find Cove for just one minute, Mom. I didn't know we were leaving now. I told him we would meet at our same spot on the beach today."

"You are not going anywhere, and not alone either. I'll go with you. Just give me one minute!"

Margaret had a way of staring into Heather's green eyes whenever Heather was about to make a wrong decision. Heather was an image of herself at that moment as she noticed how long-legged Heather was, having inherited her body type. She remembered when she was a little girl taking ballet lessons. Now she watched her daughter standing there with those same long legs. She was glad that she had taken the time to enroll her in ballet classes, hoping someday she would be onstage dancing in *The Nutcracker*.

Heather witnessing her mother rushing around packing, and then checking her watch before agreeing to go with Heather to the beach for five minutes. Margaret swallowed her anger and grabbed her beach hat. Besides Margaret's beauty, she was also a confident woman who knew what she could do. This made it easy for her to take charge of one of the stores they owned on the Jersey shore. Since Heather's dad received a degree in business management, he was very professional, which made it easy for him to be in charge of the other store. He had inherited one store when his dad had passed away. Richard and Margaret worked hard, and finally, after a few years, came across another little store just off the boardwalk. This became their second beach novelty store, which Margaret preferred to run. It was only about a mile away from their first store, so she and Richard would still meet for lunch at their favorite seafood restaurant as if it were their first date. Both stores held beach treasures like novelty toys, cups, decorations, and tiny crabs with cages. Richard and Margaret worked hard from spring through summer, which helped them to have a home of their own and enjoy their little cottage by the beach.

"Mom, please, I will be right back, I promise. I have to find Cove and show him I still have my half of the shell. I have to tell him I'm leaving and coming back. If I could tell him the number of this cottage, he'll know where to find me next time. Just let me run by myself. I'll go faster that way."

"No!" Margaret screamed, alerting Richard.

"Heather, hold on now. I'll go with you," her dad spoke with an authoritarian voice. "Even though it feels warm, you don't realize how dense the fog is out there right now."

Looking at her, he had a mental picture of when she was a very little girl hopping around the house in a tutu. His tiny dancer still ran with leaps as if on the stage. Her legs were a dancer's legs, curved from the workout of her ballet lessons. He snapped back to reality from his reminiscing as he heard the sound of the door slam. He dropped everything he was about to pack and found she was already out of the house. Heather rushed ahead, holding tight to her half of the shell as her father yelled out far behind her to slow down. His long legs pushed him into running strides trying to keep up with his daughter.

"Heather, stop! I can't keep up with you. You can't cross that street! Stop right now, I'll cross with you."

He unleashed a scream from deep inside his chest as he watched her slender body race down the street, lifting her legs high like a ballerina, just like her mother. She ran fast but with grace. His heart was racing like never before as beads of sweat dripped from his forehead, and a feeling of danger came over him. He had to reach her. Heather couldn't hear her father calling out to her; she had become completely absorbed by the thought of finding Cove. She knew she had to get to the beach and find her new friend. It was a misty, warm, early morning, and smoky haze fell onto the street, blurring her vision. Heather moved faster and with every bounce of her step found a speed in her run she had never felt before. All she could think about was her half of the shell and her new friend.

She saw the small entrance to the beach with the tapered bridge leading to the sand. Looking straight ahead, she continued to run until she heard a loud shriek pierce her ears and a shock went through her body. All went black.

Her father hovered over her as she lay in the narrow street covered by the sea mist. Her hand still grasped the shell.

Chapter 2
Memories and a Wheelchair

Years had passed since Heather's accident. The mist of the gray spring morning felt familiar to Heather. The sun seemed to purposely hide behind the dark clouds as the warm breeze flowed through her open window.

Heather rushed around her dorm kitchen getting herself ready for her morning class. Quickly filling her coffee thermos, she could hear her friend calling from outside her door. She peeked out her window and noticed a fog covering the sidewalk and street that reminded her of the dark mist that had taken her one-day years ago and the boy who remained in her heart. Then a look in the mirror made her realize her hair had a just-woken-up look. She usually didn't care much about her hair on her days off, but she realized today it needed a fix for her to look presentable for her class, so she quickly brushed her long red hair and tied it up. Then she was ready. She pushed a button, and her front door automatically opened.

Jill was calling out to Heather from the sidewalk, "Heather, come on, let's go! I don't want to be late for class!"

"This ramp is so easy to glide down! Anyone want to race?" Heather shouted as she flew down the ramp. With her arms waving high as if gliding down a roller coaster, she bellowed as her wheelchair soared like a freewheel down the steep incline.

"Heather, stop! You're being ridiculous. I can't keep up with you. Just get to the car. We have to get to class. If you keep doing this, the ramp will be taken away!"

Jill, not missing the humor, turned away and burst into laughter as she stepped into the car. Her expressive blue eyes were always inviting to people, always leading to an open discussion, as people wanted to know more about her. Her long, soft, brown hair accented her eyes, and when she smiled, there was a brightness in her face showing her cheerfulness.

Heather giggled and gave a dismissive wave. "I'm driving this time, so sit back and get ready."

Jill loved Heather's outlook on life. She always went along with one of Heather's exciting adventures. She remembered how Heather enrolled both of them in the girls' basketball team. At first, Jill didn't think it would go so well, but the team loved Heather, and they were all amazed at how she could spin on the court and get a ball in the hoop. Their shopping experiences in the mall were another escapade as Heather would keep buying at the stores and just pile up the items in her wheelchair, then speed up to the ice cream stand and treat Jill to her favorite flavor.

"What? You always drive and intentionally tease me with your wheels. You know you're faster than me! And you're the only one who can use those gadgets on the steering wheel. Don't drive with road rage, please, or I'll walk to class."

As they got ready to leave, one of the students stopped by the car and said, "Hey, girls, I see you're getting ready for class. Can I jump in, or should I sit on the roof?"

Nicky was one of their close friends and was in their English language class. He was considered to be like a brother, especially in study hall, where he would help them with their studies. His aim was to become a math teacher, so his language of numbers was a great help to them. He went to lunch or dinner with them at least every other week, and he loved Heather's natural sense of humor. He would often call Heather and have lengthy conversations and laughs.

"Sure, Nicky, jump in, or you can go into the trunk!" Heather said.

They all laughed. Because of her levity about almost any situation, especially in spite of her disability, she had drawn so many into her circle of friends, and she spread laughter all around the campus. But Jill was her anchor, her key of support, out of all of their friendships.

"I have to say, it's been a long life, a long teenage road, and now another long way till graduation. This wheelchair is my racing car and has not let me down. It's been my best friend, but of course, you're my first choice, Jill." Heather gave her a sly smile.

"Well, I'm glad to hear I'm still in the picture of your life despite that wheelchair. Have to say, though, it runs faster than me, Heather." Jill made a circular motion with her hands like wheels spinning.

Heather changed the subject. "Class has been easier than I thought. After taking all the minors, I can get to the core of my education. Even more important, I'm glad both our parents moved here to Florida where we can study at the Florida University of Marine Sciences and can remain a family," Heather said as a smile grew across her mouth.

"And to think, we'd never have met if I hadn't dragged you out from behind the pole you were hiding behind in junior high science class." Jill began to pantomime, making a shape of a pole with her hands and then pretending to peek out around it.

"Yeah, I thought you were such a nerd. I couldn't get rid of you, you followed me everywhere! But you proved your friendship to me, so that's why I didn't do away with you." Heather chuckled.

"Oh yeah, nerd yourself, I had to drag you out from behind that pole. Well, actually, I followed you from behind that pole." Jill smoothed down her shirtsleeve and gave a little shake of her shoulder in a playful motion.

"That seems such a long time ago, junior high school. Then on to high school and now look at us: in college together. You know, Jill, all joking aside, I was very lonely in junior high. So, I prayed for a friend, and that's when you came over to me after class and said hello." Heather suddenly took on a serious tone.

"Well, I told you, nerd; you can't get rid of me." Jill's eyes gave off a glassy gaze of devotion toward Heather.

"We're here. I'll Park by the ramp; it will be easier getting out." Heather turned her car into the parking space.

Nicky jumped out and started to run in the direction of his class, waving. "Thanks, girls, got to go fast! See ya later." He blew them a kiss and kept running.

Before they entered the school, Heather stopped and gave Jill a serious look. "Hey, Jill, I just wanted to say thanks for your friendship. Now let's go. I don't want to be late."

Jill smiled with her teeth shining. She knew what Heather meant. She thought of how they would debate different subjects, and whether they agreed or not, they always knew how to end their debate so it wouldn't become an argument, then go to their favorite café afterward. It was their way of maintaining the friendship. A thought came to her about a time not too long ago when they had had a heated argument about genetically modified foods.

Heather had given her a trick question to start another debate.

"Jill, let me ask you something. If you had the chance to feed the world through genetic modification, would you pursue it?"

"No, Heather, why would you even think of that? You would be tampering with the taste! Tampering with crops impacts the food chain. I can't believe you would even think of it." Jill was in shock that Heather would even bring up a subject like that since her research was in how to scientifically find healing DNA for humans and her favorites, animals.

Heather felt the tension heating up from the conversation. "Well, think of it this way. The United Nations says global food production will have to double over the next thirty-five years, so how will we feed the world?"

"In my studies, like when Brazilian nuts were crossed with soybeans, the GMOs increased resistance to antibiotics. We need antibiotics. You know that as well as I. Why are you hooked on this?" Jill now felt her friend was stirring up some fire.

"As a scientist, especially since I work with gene-splicing, etcetera, I think I would like to contribute to even more advancements. Your thinking is backward. It's not about tampering with taste. It's going beyond with introducing the increase of antioxidants to help prevent cancer or heart disease. You can't think that far!" Heather said, trying to prove her point but feeling like she was in a petty squabble.

"Natural food tastes better and is healthier for the body. I want what's natural, what comes from nature without chemicals. I'm a consumer, so I want to eat what's believed to be organic, not GMO-produced. I'm done with this conversation. We just can't seem to come to an agreement. So, let's end it now. I have to go." Jill packed up her books and jumped out of the car and went to class.

Heather got her things together, got out of the car, and went to her class alone.

After class, Jill found Heather at one of her favorite places at the study hall. She acted like there had been no argument. She invited Heather to one of their favorite cafés, and they had their favorite snacks. The conversation was not brought up again. They were back to their friendship with no questions asked. Jill was always a good listener with a calm personality and thought of Heather as humorous, and she never offended her. Jill's memory of Heather was of that morning in science class when Heather came rolling in with her wheelchair. She felt an instant connection when she saw her feisty way of entering the class. They felt free to speak honestly with each other and always respected each other's views. By not having siblings, they became sisters, which made their parents as close as family. The families joked that even though they were sisters by choice, they never had to fight about the chore list since they lived in separate houses.

Their friendship had started with open hearts sharing and caring for each other's lives. Since they had no siblings between them, they had learned to accept each other's personalities and temperaments. Heather always had a quick reply to any question or remark from Jill. She appreciated that Jill accepted her boldness and wit. Heather had trusted Jill from the beginning when they had first met in junior high. She remembered how Jill had tried so hard to make friends. She enjoyed that memory, and she put on a little grin of delight. She thought, *Junior High was so long ago, it was a good time of making friends with Jill.*

Chapter 3
Finding Friends

It was a brisk September morning and the first day of junior high for Jill. She nervously looked out the sliding door to their wooded deck. She loved growing up in Point Pleasant, New Jersey, where there was always a scent of the ocean. It flowed through the screen door as she waited for her mom to get ready to drive her to her new school.

Elementary school had been easy for Jill because she had had lots of friends, but now that they all were enrolled in private school, she felt left out of their lives. Turning thirteen and being a teenager with a new move into a public junior high school was troubling to her. She felt like she would never have friends like the ones she had before. She sat at the kitchen table, flipping her spoon after each bite of her yogurt and feeling overwhelmed.

Her mom, Jillian, called out to her as she ran down the long oak staircase of their center hall Colonial, "Jill, stop. You're getting the yogurt all over the table." She placed her lunch bag on the counter and quickly filled her thermos with her coffee and favorite vanilla creamer, then grabbed a banana to go with her favorite lunch sandwich, peanut butter and jelly. She placed it all in her lunch bag, grabbed her quilted Gucci shoulder bag and her car keys, and turned to her daughter. "Come on, Jill, let's get into the car. I have to go now!"

Jill was still flipping the spoon. "Yeah, okay, Mom. I wish I didn't have to start school yet. I'm not ready. I lost all my friends. I still don't understand why I couldn't go with all of them to the private school that they're attending. I'm not going to know anyone in this junior high."

Jillian saw the look on her daughter's face, so she stopped and sat down next to her. "Listen, when I was young, my parents decided to sell the house, so I had to move to a new town and go to a new school. Junior high was difficult for me. I felt like a fish out of water. It was also my fault. I could have been friendlier, but I wasn't. I became a little depressed. Then, one day, one girl out of the entire class sat next to me during lunch. You know her as Aunt Josie. She's been my friend ever since. So, making life changes isn't easy, but before you know it, you'll have a bunch of friends."

She covered Jill's hand with hers and continued talking. "Once you realize that school friends become your second family—you eat together, laugh together, and learn together—you'll get more comfortable. Don't worry, Jill, it really will pass quickly. I can't wait to hear you ask me if you can go out with your friends. Now let's get going. I have a couple of houses to show to my clients. And don't forget to finish your homework so we can have a leisurely dinner with your dad tonight. He's always so busy at his office, but tonight he'll be home earlier than usual and looking forward to sitting down together as a family," Jillian said with a little laugh and a nod to move out.

Standing tall and lean, wearing a mint-green suit, she grabbed her filled bags and, with the sound of her clicking heels, she started for the door.

"Yeah, yeah, yeah, okay, I'm ready. I really don't want to be late for this great new experience." She gave her mother a sneering look, then quickly jumped up from the chair, grabbed her backpack, and followed her to the door.

Their home was a real estate dream, with vaulted ceilings and floor-to-ceiling windows like a glass wall. Jill's elementary school friends had looked forward to their sleepovers since her room was like an oversize master bedroom. The girls would put sleeping bags and pillows all over the floor. Sodas and bowls of snacks would fill their bellies as they watched all their favorite shows on Jill's large television. Summertime had been especially fun for the girls. After Jill's mom made a special breakfast for them, they would spend the afternoon in Jill's in-ground pool. Jill had had lots of friends, some from the neighborhood but mainly the girls from school she had grown up with. She had felt life was so good.

Her parents always gave dinner parties. Hired servers would move wordlessly through the rooms dressed in white tunics and white gloves moving all around the long dining table, keeping the platters and glasses full. Jill's parents did lots of entertaining with her dad's office friends and her mom's real estate coworkers. There was always soft music, hazy chatter, and laughter when filling the house with their guests. There were many weekend parties and festivities in this Point Pleasant dream estate where Jill and her parents felt united in many ways and where contentment filled their lives.

Jill's parents were high school sweethearts. Jillian remembered the first time she noticed Jeff. It was the first day of high school. She was the first student to arrive to math class. She watched as each student entered and found a seat. Then Jeff walked in with his thick, dark-brown, wavy hair. She thought, *He walks in as if he thinks he's a god, but I like his bright blue eyes. I wonder if he will notice me.*

As he took his seat just a row away from her, he looked up and noticed her long, soft, brown hair reaching down to her waist. She turned around to look at him, and their eyes connected.

After class, he walked over to her. "Hi, my name is Jeff." He stood there a little embarrassed and lost for words.

"Well, hello. My name is Jillian. I noticed you as soon as you walked in. Want to meet up after school?" She wanted to make her move really quickly because he was standing there frozen.

He hesitated for a moment. "Ah…oh yeah…sure. Everyone goes to the coffee shop at the mall. Meet you there?"

"K, see you there." She moved out of the class and on to her next one. She knew if she played it cool, he would want to see her.

From their first September date amid the autumn colors of golden leaves, their hands never let go. Their favorite spot was a bench under the maple tree in the nearby park. They would run through the colorful leaves and fall into a pile. Their first kiss felt like a cozy blanket under the leaves. Their love grew from the sweetness of summer through autumn and into the snowy winter days. And every season was a season of beauty to them. Every day was a treasure.

Jeff and Jillian graduated high school together. They both attended the local community college where Jeff received his bachelor's and master's degrees in accounting and business administration, respectively. Jillian received a Bachelor of Science degree for business administration in banking and finance. She acquired an in-depth understanding of financial statements, market trends, and statistical analysis. Jeff was able to start his own business as a tax accountant, and Jillian worked for a while as a market research analyst helping a local company promote their productions. She would gather data from software companies and analyze then convert the findings into understandable tables, graphs, and written reports for her clients to help the company market its product. During the first year of their professions, they were able to save their money and lower their college debt. They looked forward to their future together.

They married a year later and settled into their new home in Point Pleasant. Then the joy of having their first child, Jill, who was named after her mother, was like a gift, a little pink package that grabbed their hearts. That was when Jillian decided to become a broker and opened her own real estate office so she would have more time at home with her daughter. Life was good for them. They were rooted in the soil of family, nurturing one another and loving their life. They enjoyed watching their daughter grow into each year of school, from kindergarten, through junior high school, high school and college. The years passed quickly.

***

Jill's first day at school began, and she became a little more comfortable after a few morning classes helped her learn the ropes. She thought, *So this is where I get to meet my other family. I'll become part of a new tribe, like Mom said.* She found herself traveling through what felt like a maze of hallways filled with the echoes of a thousand noisy voices from students in every direction. Finally, she matched the room number on her student class card with the science room and with an exhale of her breath walked in.

There was just one seat left, in the back of the class. If she got there quickly, nobody would have time to notice how nervous she was. Most of the students were in the front of the class and there was no one next to her, so she felt she could relax and breathe. She quietly sat and took out her notebook and watched what the other students were doing. Science was her favorite subject, which made it easier for her to transition from all the other morning classes, and she couldn't wait to take her lunch break, which was right after her next class.

Then she saw the girl in the wheelchair. Jill watched her struggle to find a place to fit in, finally pushing chairs aside and settling into a place behind a divider pole. Jill was amazed that someone could wheel about so boldly. She thought, *I like her. She looks like nothing bothers her. I wonder if she would even care to make friends.*

As the minutes of the lesson passed, the bell rang, and the ceaseless buzzing of the classroom became louder as desks and chairs were pushed aside for the great escape into the hallway. Then Jill ran through some of the students blocking her way just in time as Heather was packing up her books.

"Hi, my name is Jill. I'm new here. What's yours?"

"My name is Heather. What's up? What do you want?" she answered, a little annoyed.

"Actually, I want to make new friends. Everyone here is so new, no one wants to talk to me." Jill gazed down at Heather with a pleading expression in her eyes.

"Well, yeah, that's true. We all come from different parts of this community. I went to elementary school across town. Where did you go?"

"Oh, the school just one mile from here. I live close to this part of town."

"So, what's your schedule? Let me see your program card. Oh, look at this—we have the same lunch break. I'll meet you there. We can sit together, if you like." Heather handed back the class card with a firm look on her face.

Jill smiled widely. "I'm on my way to math now, so yes, I'll meet you in the lunchroom right after that. So come on, let's go, come out from behind that pole!" she said jokingly.

"Okay, it's set. I'm on my way to English now, so I'll see you next period in the lunchroom. Okay, then get out of my way, and I'm not hiding behind this pole!"

Then Heather quickly pushed her way to the elevator.

Heather studied hard in her English class, but she preferred science and looked forward to taking more in-depth science in high school. Her cherished ambition was to find a college where she could use science to make a difference in the world. She thought of human life and its struggles, like herself in a wheelchair. The thought of all kinds of health issues, the environment, and air quality. Then her thoughts turned to the ocean and the life it held, and all the shells she remembered on the beach where she vacationed and that one particular shell.

Finally, the break came. Heather went to the cafeteria and got seated with her lunch. She waved to Jill. Jill waved back, then came and sat across from her. She noticed a lunchroom sign with rules.

1. STAY IN YOUR SEAT.
2. TALK QUIETLY.
3. EAT YOUR OWN FOOD.
4. CLEAN UP YOUR MESS.
5. BE KIND.

She covered her ears for a moment to block the chatter of the masses sitting and devouring their lunches. Then she moved her hand to her nose to hold back the smell of the mixture of sweet and spicy aromas pouring from the kitchen.

"You got out early and found a table for us?" Jill guessed as she unpacked her sandwich.

"I leave five minutes earlier before class ends so I can get to the elevator and get down here for my lunch. I don't have to deal with the crowds passing in the halls. Convenient for me, right?" Heather's eyes stared into Jill's, waiting for more questions, especially about her wheelchair.

"Yes, I think that's a good idea for you. It's like a mass stampede in these halls. I don't like it. I miss elementary school. The halls in this school are so much busier, the students seem less friendly, and no one cares that I don't know my way around. I was so glad to hear the bell ring so

I was free from math class to get here with you." Jill nervously twirled her long, brown hair around her finger.

"Yeah, right, I'm surprised you didn't need a map to get here," Heather said, laughing. "It's my first day also, just like everyone else here, so don't let it get to you. Before you know it, this day will be over, and then the whole year will be done. How do you like that one?" She laughed again, folding her arms as she sat back.

Jill had a pleasant disposition and always had a twinkle in her eyes, especially now when making a new friend. "That's true. I guess I'm overthinking all of this. Thanks for the encouragement."

"By the way, before the bell rings, do you have any questions about my wheelchair before lunch is over?" Heather asked in a strong voice.

Jill was stunned, and it must have shown on her face, because Heather laughed.

"Wow, Heather, I didn't expect that," Jill managed. "Of course, I wondered why, but I really don't even care about that; it's your friendship I care about."

"Just testing you. Maybe someday I'll tell you about it," Heather said with a sharp glance.

"Well, lunch is just about over. I won't see you in the next class. We can exchange numbers and keep in touch if you want to."

Heather examined Jill's face to see if she really wanted to be friends.

"Yes, I'd love to. Here's mine. Call me when you get home. Okay? By the way, I was only ten when I was in an accident."

The two girls had no way of knowing this was the beginning of a lifelong friendship and a magical journey into their shared future.

Chapter 4
Learning to Live

The windows of the hospital room were so large that the glare of sunlight bounced off the steel bed, touching Heather's eyes. She was startled by loud voices that echoed through her head. She slowly opened her eyes and found herself staring at an arrangement of gray, square tiles with an odor of bleach. Then she realized she was staring at the floor. She couldn't move her neck, and there was a warm, weighted feeling on her chest and back that ran down her body. Then a clear baritone voice reverberated through the room.

"Good morning, Heather. I'm glad you are finally awake. My name is Dr. Wallace. I am the chief neurosurgeon here in this hospital."

He then rolled over a small black rolling stool and sat close to her, leaning a little toward her as she remained in the same face-down position in the Stryker traction frame. A nurse also sat by and caressed Heather's small hand to help her not to be fearful.

"Heather, dear, you were in a terrible accident. I thought it best for now that you stay in this position; it will help you to get better. The nurses here will always be by your side.

Don't be afraid; we will take care of you. Your parents are waiting outside your room. I'll go get them now." The doctor softly patted her head to give her some type of comfort as he left the room.

Heather couldn't move. Her brain tried to register what she had just been told. She started counting her tears as they fell onto the tiles.

The waiting room was a little down the hall from Heather's room. It appeared to be freshly painted white. The seats were gray material and were comfortable. Richard and Margaret held hands for emotional support while waiting for the doctor. They wished they could turn back time to that day on the beach. They would have gone to the boardwalk instead of rushing to pack the car. There would not have been an accident; there would not have been a hit and run car accident with their daughter. If only someone would have witnessed and come forward with the identification. But even that would not have spared Heather's condition. Just at that moment the doctor walked into the room with the posture of a soldier in his formal white coat. He spoke with a cold and distant tone; the way professionals do. His face showed the emotion of being glum, but when he looked into the eyes of Heather's parents, the tone of his voice became warm while he spoke about the situation. As he held Heather's medical file in his hands, he explained her condition with empathy.

"Please allow me to sit here with you, Mr. and Mrs. Storm. I would like to explain your daughter's condition. Heather has a spinal cord injury that has severed the connections between her brain and her extremities. She has severe thoracic damage to the cervical area. She may have lost all function below that area. The motor connections to her legs have been wiped out. Also, there are two crushed vertebrae in her neck. The vehicle that struck her snapped all the ligaments and tendons in her neck, allowing a couple of the vertebra to pound the delicate nerve tissue. She must remain in the Stryker frame to stabilize the injury; this could take up to seven weeks. This hospital specializes in this type of injury. The nurses here are trained to work with patients in this condition. The routine will be to turn her without disrupting the traction. Any disturbance can have extremely negative consequences. But it also helps in preventing bed sores.

This situation will not end anytime soon. After the seven weeks, she will have to remain in rehabilitation and receive physical therapy."

In that moment, the room became soundless. There were no thoughts of yesterday or tomorrow. They stared into his darkened eyes with horror and tried to listen, almost as if he were speaking another language. Then, with a shaky voice, Margaret desperately asked one question.

"Will she walk?"

Richard held his breath. He sensed the answer of his daughter's outcome would not be good.

"Mr. and Mrs. Storm, there is a very strong chance that the injury may result in partial or total paralysis of all four limbs and torso. We will not know for sure until the seven weeks have passed. Furthermore, with all the physical therapy she will receive, it's possible that she will use her upper limbs, but I'm not sure of her torso and legs. I am terribly sorry for this young child. But please have faith for her."

The doctor leaned toward them and held them for a moment, then quickly rose and guided them to Heather's room. There was a sound in their heads as though thunder had cracked the sky with the news the doctor had given them. As they walked into the room, they held back their inner screams of fear and heartbreak and fell to their knees to look upward into their daughter's face. With Heather's tears falling onto their faces and melding with theirs, they feared their family's life had been destroyed.

***

Heather's parents stayed at the hospital day and night. Since the Hospital for Neurosurgery was in a nearby town of New Jersey, it wasn't far to travel from their home. It seemed to Heather that one of her parents was always in the room with her, holding her hand or praying for her.

"Lord, you have love for all your creations. You created Heather for us. She is your child. Comfort her for what she must endure. Heal her. Let her walk. Bring her back to the beach where she can play like a child again." There was a tiny flicker of hope in their hearts as they lifted their heads upward as they ended their daily prayer.

Although Heather was just ten years old, she understood that a car accident had almost taken her life. Lying in the Stryker frame, she had plenty of time to think. She felt very tired, wanting so much to get out of the traction, which felt tight across her body. And at times she remembered an ear-piercing sound that had struck her and then waking up to voices talking over her body.

She thought to herself, *I'm so scared, and I don't know if I can ever walk again. I want to go home. Does Cove know what happened? Does he know where I am, or is he looking for me? Where is the shell he gave me?*

There was the sound of wheels as hospital beds rolled past her that she couldn't see and the sound of chatter coming from the nurses' station. Daytime folded into nighttime as she counted each time the sunrays came through the window, waiting for time to pass. Then the day arrived when she was taken out of traction and began physical therapy.

Nancy entered Heather's room and watched as the nurses had just finished adjusting and turning Heather on the Stryker frame.

"Hi, Heather, my name is Nancy, and I'm your private physical therapist. Today, we'll take you off the Stryker frame and bring you in one of our therapy rooms, and there you will begin an intense program of therapy. I want you to understand that this will help you reach your maximum potential. We will help you to strengthen your muscle mass and improve your cardiovascular health. Are you ready for some of this action?" Nancy tried to help Heather embrace a positive attitude, hoping this would help her progress during all the difficulty she was about to face.

Heather felt Nancy's encouraging, positive energy. Just being freed from the traction had given her hope. She couldn't wait to start. Her heart beat a little faster as she thought, *I will walk again, I will run again, I will dance.*

"Well, now, let me think about it. Just kidding! I'm so happy to get out of that traction. Now I can see everything

41

right side up. And that dull, gray floor with the bleach smell, yuk! Yeah, I'm ready!"

Heather was now placed on a tilt table for ten days for her circulation and to slowly get used to the pressure of being upright. She was now able to see her treasure chest of doctors, physical therapists, and nurses. Now she connected their voices to their faces.

"Nancy, I knew you had brown hair. I just thought of you that way." She giggled. "And Dr. Wallace, I kinda figured you wore glasses." Her giggle turned to loud laughter as she pointed to him. Even Dr. Wallace smiled from ear to ear.

Each day, Heather was raised a couple of inches at a time. She sometimes felt nauseous, but knew that someday soon she would be at a full standing position and ready for the wheelchair. There were times that she would cry a little, but when she noticed some children at about her age being wheeled past her, she thought, *They made it through that traction, and now some are using the wheelchair and some are walking with help. I can do this!*

Her flexibility and range of motion improved daily with the strenuous routine of exercise. Heather felt sore after each session.

"Nancy, does it have to hurt so much after this therapy?"

Nancy explained that her muscles required stretching and exercise in order for her to be able to move her arms again. Heather understood and wanted to move her arms and legs like she had seen when the children had passed by her the other day. She wanted to join them one day. She just wanted this stretching to be over with. Nancy's skilled hands used movements intended to produce a strong effect on Heather's neck and arms in the hopes that she would soon be able to lift a spoon to her mouth. She would show Heather how to push her arms against hers for resistance to improve muscle activation.

"Heather, let me take your wrist and guide your hands with the fork as I assist you with this movement. You will be able to try it on your own very soon."

There was much improvement within a couple of weeks. Heather felt so independent in being able to pick up her utensils to eat. Nancy never left her side. She enjoyed watching Heather improve by eating her meals without assistance.

She became one of the most loved children in the therapy sessions. Physical and occupational therapists worked with her and spent time with her during her lunch and dinner. Her outlook on her life situation became cheerful, and all the hospital staff found her humor delightful.

Heather giggled loudly. "Okay, Nancy, keep pulling my arms and legs. Maybe you can make me taller!"

Nancy tickled Heather's arms and laughed, and the nurses close by stopped what they were doing just to see Heather laughing.

"Heather, your giggles are contagious. You have all of us laughing," said one of the nurses who would purposely try to be nearby when Heather was in therapy. She loved that Heather would ask questions or would joke in her silly manner and make them all laugh.

Nancy smiled and squeezed Heather's arms as she helped her into her wheelchair. "You are stronger now, so I can start you on the activity arch. I think you will enjoy it.

It will help you to develop gross motor skills. We need to strengthen those arm muscles."

Heather giggled with her silly laughter. "Okay, I'm ready. Back on to my wheels. I can't wait to do the aquatic exercises! When can I start that?"

"I have your schedule ready for you, and aquatic exercise is in three days, so give yourself time, little one," Nancy replied with a smile and adoring eyes.

It was a daily activity for Heather. The physical therapy room was filled with all types of equipment to help children regain their strength, from activity frames, weight machines, and seated aquatic exercises to leg lifts, ankle pump exercises, and rowing machines. And finally, the aquatic pool. Heather's eyes widened with wonder at the size; to her, it was like the ocean.

"You're a strong little girl; I see such improvement in your upper body. I'm so proud of you." Nancy gave her a wink and a quick hug.

"Thanks, Nancy. The aquatic pool really helped more than anything, don't you think? Oh, I just love the water, and I love the feeling of floating. It's so much fun. Maybe I can swim like a fish. I love swimming!"

"Well, then, how about you trying to swim like a mermaid right now? I'll hold on to the hoist lift once we get you into that pool. You can use your arms and try to use your legs. Good exercise for you, my little fish. And you will be the most beautiful mermaid in our ocean." Nancy smiled and laughed, enjoying her time with Heather.

"I love the ocean and the little creatures that live there; I wish I could swim with them. My parents would take me to the Jersey shore every summer. We would swim and play in the sand. Then I met a boy there, and we ran up and down the sand. We collected sea glass and seashells. It was so much fun. Do you think someday I could go back there?"

Nancy noticed that Heather's legs had some muscle tone even though she couldn't move. "Heather, you have a strong, positive personality and very strong legs. You will go back to the beach. You must have done a lot of swimming. Your legs show some muscle strength."

"Oh, that's because my mom always took me to ballet class, and Dad installed a ballet barre for me to practice every day. I'll go back to my classes as soon as I'm better."

Heather's memory kept repeating her time at the beach and swimming in the ocean with her family. How her father would lift her in the air and drop her in the ocean, then swim alongside her. She thought that was how she had learned to swim. She had sandwiches and a cold drink while sitting on the beach blanket, then a short rest time and back to the water. Then another snack break after a swim in the ocean, where her dad would bring her an ice cream cone. She could feel the cold ice cream dripping down her chin. Then she thought about how her mom would use the ballet barre with her and tell her stories of when she was young and danced on the stage. She wanted to be just like her since she had been a ballerina at one time. She could still see the sunflowers growing in the front yard, which was her parents' symbol of their first meeting and had also become her favorite flower. And then there was the memory of running with Cove, filling their bucket with the seashells and then finding that one special shell, the one whose half he had given to her.

"Well, Heather, keep that in mind. When you grow older, you might be able to do just that." Nancy wanted her words to give Heather the hope she was secretly holding in her own heart.

Heather laughed. Then her watery eyes enlarged with a question. "Nancy, did I have a shell in my hand when I came here?"

Nancy stuttered for a moment, then placed her hand over Heather's. "Yes, I do remember a shell. Your parents took it. You can ask them; they will be here any minute. I'm sure it's safe."

It seemed like yesterday that she had been on the beach. For Heather, her life moved forward from yesterday's memories of the girl on the beach meeting her first love and on to what tomorrow held for her.

***

Richard and Margaret felt like their world was slowly disappearing as they spent so much time looking for the shell that they had long forgotten about. Since Margaret was always tidy and well organized, from her manicured fingers to her clothes and hair, she always made sure to keep everything under control. She took pride in her house and in the little cottage they owned by the beach. She thought she had organized the attic, but as they climbed up the attic staircase, they realized it hadn't been touched in a year. While she brushed off the fine dust that lay on top of boxes stored away with some of Heather's toys, a heavy thought came to her that Heather would never play with them again.

Like a child peeking through a cracked door, she carefully searched for the missing shell. As she knelt by the boxes in the attic, her whole body shook, and she could feel the pounding of her heart against her rib cage.

"Oh, Richard, what if we can't find that shell? I must have broken it into pieces or threw it out. I was in such a shock that night, I just don't remember." Her voice quivered as she tried to force each word while trying to catch her breath.

Richard held Margaret in his arms, comforting her and himself as well.

"I know, Margaret. I can't believe after all this time she still remembered that shell! I really was hoping she had forgotten about it. Such a smart little girl, she never forgets anything. We have to find it!"

"I do remember that night we came home from the hospital. We were both in such shock, I took the bag from the hospital and just threw it up here. I didn't even think of checking inside for anything. It was like my mind was saying, 'Her life is over; my life is done.' I never want to look in that hospital bag again. I know how you feel. I felt so sick deep in my stomach, so deep in my heart. I feel like my baby girl is trapped in that frame. Her life has changed forever, and so has ours."

With glassy eyes, he crouched in another corner of the attic as his dark eyes shed a tear. He wiped it away as he watched his wife rummage through boxes and thought how strong her resemblance to their daughter was. He was glad she hadn't inherited his dark hair and eyes. Although he was a handsome man, he felt somewhat too tall for his build. He crouched on one side of the attic so as to not hit his head on the wood beam. That was when he wished he were a couple of inches shorter.

"Margaret, I always wanted to have a dormer on this side of the attic. There's certainly plenty of room for it. I don't know if it matters at this point."

A few moments later, Richard noticed something in the far end of the attic. "Wait, I think I found something. Yes, here's the brown bag I brought up here after we left the emergency room!" he cried out from the other side of the room.

Richard was able to stand in the middle of the attic and made his way over to where Margaret sat. They sat together on the hardwood floor and opened the bag. Inside, they found a clear, closed hospital bag with Heather's name printed on it. Inside was the gold necklace she had worn that morning. Margaret remembered when she had given it to their daughter for her tenth birthday. They also found her little birthstone ring and the white summer shirt she had worn that day. Margaret thought she had rummaged through all the things in the bag when she felt something hard but smooth with a little point at the end. She pulled out the seashell with its irradiant shine like when it was first found.

"Richard, look, here it is, still has a shine to it." Then handed it over to her husband.

Richard sat holding up the shell and all of Heather's little items.

"Oh, Richard, there's a silence in my soul now. I haven't slept since all this happened. I feel like I'm living in a dead, cold winter, locked away in a cabin that I can't escape."

Then she took the shell from Richard's hand and held it up, turning it around as if looking for an answer. "Maybe the shell will give her hope." She bent her head in disbelief and cried.

"Wait, I have an idea! It's right in front of me bigger than life." Richard became fascinated with his idea. He laid down the gold chain against the shell and rubbed his chin.

"Here it is," he said. "We'll have our jeweler connect these two pieces and make a necklace for Heather. What do you think?" He moved closer to his wife and put his arm around her, patting her shoulder.

"Oh, Richard, this makes me so happy. Imagine how she will feel when she sees this." They fell into each other's arms, crying tears of pain and joy.

The next morning, after a quick stop at the jeweler, Richard and Margaret had the surprise for Heather.

As they entered her room, they stood there and watched her sitting up in her comfort chair talking to Nancy. It was a feeling of great loss; their world had given way to any of life's pleasures they had hoped to live, and it now turned in horror. Margaret thought, *How do I describe this heartache? Just watching her now is like hearing music that has lost its notes.*

"Heather, my little girl, here is a surprise for you." Richard's face beamed as he handed her a square, velvet box.

Heather's face turned to her dad in surprise. "Hi, Dad, Mom, I didn't see you. I'm so busy talking to Nancy, I didn't even hear you."

She took the box and slowly opened it. Then, with a joyous squeal and tears in her eyes, she held up the necklace.

"Oh, Dad, you found it! I knew I still had it somewhere. And you made it a necklace?"

Heather was now able to move her arms with strength and placed the gold necklace over her head. It rested perfectly around her neck. As her fingers touched the shell, giving her a deep image of the boy on the beach, she whispered, "Cove."

The hospital felt like a new home for Richard and Margaret with the constant back-and-forth and even some nights where one of them was offered a bed to sleep over with their daughter. Dr. Wallace had another meeting with them. The doctor made sure to keep in touch weekly about Heather's progress. He had grown fond of her and her parents and looked forward to giving them the great updates of Heather's developments.

"The plan of progress I have set for Heather seems to be working. Her attitude during this time has helped her to have a favorable outcome. Plus, I noticed right away what a happy little girl Heather is, but lately, she's seemed even more joyful and has worked even harder, almost as if something triggered her emotions and moved over her body and soul."

Something silently flashed between Richard and Margaret. With a quick look into each other's eyes and almost an invisible nod, they acknowledged knowing their daughter had grown stronger once her hands had held the shell.

Margaret thought back to how she had met Richard, just a couple of years after her accident at her recital rehearsal. It was a time she could never forget. She had that slight limp to remind her. But the memory of her life on the stage, with all the pliés and pointe work, was her world. Through the blisters and calluses, she fought each day to continue. Her beauty was like a diamond created by God, and her passion made her float effortlessly across the stage. The brightness within her shone outward through her eyes as she lifted both arms and gracefully stretched them above her head. She elegantly continued without any pauses until a sudden change to the grand jeté. She rose in the air for just a moment until her landing caused a dancer's fracture.

At first, it was just an ankle sprain that slowly grew into stress fractures and, finally, long-term foot damage. Surgery ended all aspirations of France and her vision of becoming a famous danseuse. Her beauty remained, but with each simple step she took, her gait reminded her of a dream she had once held in her heart.

A couple of years later, she took a job as a clothes retailer because she had finally accepted that she would never dance again. This one warm summer day, she decided to drive to the beach and just sit and relax. She passed a flower shop and thought it would be nice to browse and find her favorite flower. She passed by so many, taking in each scent. And then she saw them, standing tall in a long, glass floor jar. Sunflowers. She picked one up and examined the round flower head. It was perfect. Then she heard a voice that startled her.

"Excuse me, you like sunflowers? Do you know the meaning behind them?"

"Oh, I do know. Besides their beauty, they are also known for being happy flowers." She stepped back, feeling a little uncomfortable talking to a stranger.

"I didn't mean to startle you. My name is Richard. I own the little novelty store by the beachfront. I actually sell sunflower seeds. I'm browsing too, looking for a bouquet for my mother." He was captured by her beauty, her green eyes, and her red hair. He wanted to say more.

"Oh, you live here in Point Pleasant? So, do I. I usually go a different way but decided to drive where I can park and not walk so much. I'd like to see your store and what you're selling and maybe buy some seeds for my backyard." She became somewhat interested in him, with his dark, coffee-colored eyes, which she thought were mysterious looking.

"Sure, if you want, you can follow my car and I'll take you to a small parking lot where you can park and walk in the store. I think you will enjoy what's in there. By the way, what's your name?" His eyebrows arched in a questioning way.

"Oh, silly me. My name is Margaret. Glad to meet you." She stretched out her hand to shake his, and a feeling of comfort and reassurance went through her. She felt his hand was like a warm glove.

When she entered the store, she found it to be very interesting. There were beach-themed coffee cups, beach towels, beach balls, surfboards. There was a section for kids displaying puzzles, beach buckets, and sandcastle forms. She enjoyed watching the tiny crabs with colorful shells in a cage. She giggled at the sight of the seahorses in the glass fish tank. Then she found a large selection of seed packets. She chose a few, then found the sunflower seeds. She went to the counter and was ready to pay for her items.

"Here you go, Richard. I'm so glad I met you and found your store. So much to see in here! Well, I found more seeds than I thought I would need, especially my favorite."

She paid and was ready to leave when he nervously called out to her.

"Oh, aah, b-b-by the way, s-s-sunflowers also s-s-signify adoration because they turn to face the sun as a sign of d-d-dedication. T-t-thought you might enjoy t-t-that explanation." He felt his face redden as he stuttered out the words. He hoped they would talk some more.

She turned to him as she reached for the door and said, "That is very interesting. Thanks for the information. Maybe I'll stop by tomorrow."

While she sat in her car, she thought, *He's very handsome and very tall. I would like to get to know him.*

After a couple of days, she went back to the store and invited him for coffee. They went for a coffee break along the boardwalk. Sitting at a table overlooking the ocean, they talked about their lives.

"This little novelty store was my father's. As a child, I would always help out in the store. Sometimes I would get lost in my imagination in the back of the store, playing with all the empty boxes. I was just a kid and thought someday I would be an astronaut as I threw my toy figures up into the air. They would land on an empty box I had painted. I tried to make it look like the moon. But you can imagine what it really looked like." He sat shaking his head and laughing.

"Well, that's what kids do, right? I was taught ballet lessons at a young age. Then after college, I was accepted in the American Ballet Theatre, so all my thoughts went into dancing onstage at Lincoln Center. Then one day as I was practicing for the recital with my troupe, my dreams were shattered. I fractured my ankle. I've never walked the same again." She hung her head.

"Margaret, I'm sorry. But maybe someday you will have a daughter, and you can teach her how to be a ballerina, to engage in a safer way of dancing. It will all work out. You wait and see." Richard leaned over and held her hand.

Soon after their first coffee date, they began meeting for dinner. They met every Friday night and during the week. They enjoyed theme parks and roller-coaster rides and always ended the date with ice cream sundaes. Their relationship became more serious, and they were thrilled to be together.

After a few months, on this one particular night at their usual dinner on the boardwalk at their favorite seafood restaurant, Richard handed her a bunch of sunflowers.

"Oh, Richard, this is beautiful. You're so sweet. You know my favorite flowers. My sunflowers!"

Then she felt a pink silk ribbon tying them together. As her fingers traced the ribbon, she felt something unusual. When she looked down at the ribbon, there was an engagement ring tied with a bow to the ribbon.

"Richard, a ring!" Her heart was racing as she watched him untie the ring.

He knelt, holding the ring in one hand and her hand with his other. "Margaret, will you marry me?"

"Yes, Richard, yes!"

They clung together on the boardwalk by the ocean, feeling deep love for each other and knowing they were meant to be together.

***

Their life was an exciting journey. As they were driving toward the beach one day, they spotted a house for sale not far from Richard's store. They walked in and immediately fell in love with it. They decided to arrange a wedding date for that summer. It was late July on the beach when they took their vows on a warm summer evening.

After a couple of years, they were able to open a second store. Business was booming, and they were able to buy a summer home. It was a little Cape Cod, and Margaret was sure to plant her favorite sunflowers at both homes. Its similar look to their home was why they had decided to rent it. When the owner of the home gave them the option to buy, it was an immediate yes. Their home had a strong resemblance to the cottage they rented each summer. The white window shutters had red rose vines climbing up the side of the house and a section where sunflowers grew as tall as the second floor.

Soon after setting up their homes, they experienced the joy of having a child: Heather was born.

When Heather turned three years old, Margaret enrolled in 'Mommy and Me' classes to get her started in dance movements. Then they went to creative movement classes, which finally brought Heather to ballet classes. Margaret watched her daughter learn how to balance, skip, and leap to the music. By the time Heather was ten, she could move very elegantly with her long legs. Margaret and Richard had a ballet barre installed in their family room and attended each recital. Watching her daughter brought back all the memories of her love for ballet, but now she was hoping her daughter would be the one to succeed where she felt she had failed. Margaret lived vicariously through Heather, reliving her love for this art. Her daughter would be a ballerina. She would dance.

***

Chapter 5
Onward and Travels

Cove pursued a rigorous combination for a premed major course in his high school. He studied hard at physics and chemistry and acquired the highest grades possible. Not only did he spend time at his studies, he also was involved in the basketball league in his school and the town baseball league, where his peers valued his friendship.

Cove knew that when he went to college, he was going to miss his home, where he and his dad Joseph would play baseball in their huge backyard. He remembered that from elementary school and up to high school, his mom made sure to fill the refrigerator with sodas and snacks for the Friday night youth group meetings they would host for their church at least twice a month. The basement was a special treat for him, where he would invite his friends over and they would play ping-pong and eat all the popcorn while watching their favorite videos on the television screen his dad had installed. Their home was like a mansion to Cove, filled with fun and lots of love.

He enjoyed their family travels to Manhattan on the ferry service for special occasions, like celebrating one of their birthdays or a holiday. They took pleasure in the sights of the tall buildings. Their favorite was the Flatiron Building. They loved the triangular shape, and Cove would always try to count the windows in a row to reach the top. He loved munching on the street vendors' supplies of snacks. His favorite was the roasted chestnuts. They reminded him of Christmas. Each year, they would purchase tickets for the newest theatrical play. But they always made sure to make a special trip just before Christmas to see their old-time favorite, *A Christmas Carol*, then take a walk around Rockefeller Center's Christmas tree. The ending of their evening would be to walk Forty-Second Street and have a dinner at a special restaurant and then ice cream for dessert. With all the suspense and thrill of the Manhattan experience, Cove often felt that one day he would somehow be a part of the Big Apple. He thought, *Maybe someday, if I become successful in my future, I can buy an apartment right here in New York!*

Another one of their favorite places was to take a ferry ride to Fire Island and spend the day enjoying homemade ice cream and sit in the pavilion and watch the waves. They would have great conversations about Cove's future, and his dad would tell him stories of fishermen and all about marine life.

"Dad, what about the old myths about mermaids? Could they be true?"

"Son, I teach science and biology, and I have never come across facts that they exist, but it is good for the imagination."

Mary said with delight, "Cove, with those long fingers, you could be a surgeon or pianist in a live orchestra!"

"Talk about imagination. But great thoughts for our son, dear," his dad said with deep pleasure and admiration.

They all laughed some belly laughs and enjoyed the ocean view.

But they all agreed that even though they loved their outings to Fair Harbor Beach, Fire Island, didn't compare to their rental cottage at Holgate on the Jersey shore. When Cove was just about a year old, it was a place they had spent many summers at their favorite rental cottage, which was only two blocks from the entrance of the beach. Cove remembered the concession stand was filled with all kinds of trinkets, snacks, and his favorite swirl ice cream. It felt more like home to Cove, where he felt so comfortable sitting on the beach blanket with his parents, feeling the ocean breeze and smelling the ocean's scent.

This one particular Saturday morning, there was the fragrance of blueberries that brought Cove to the kitchen. Still a little drowsy, he leaned on the kitchen table, resting his head in his hand while he watched his mom making his favorite blueberry pancakes, and he thought, *This is the perfect time to talk to her about what has been weighing on my mind. I really hope she is willing to listen and understand.*

"Mom, I've been thinking about all the summer camps I went to. They were all lots of fun, bonfires, rock climbing, even the zip lines, but that was all when I was in junior high school. I need something different while I'm in high school." He sat tapping his fingers on the table, waiting for her to drill him as she always did.

"Sure, Cove, what were you thinking would be a different camp during this summer while in high school?" She smiled at him as she as she served his hot pancakes, and she looked into his full brown chestnut-color eyes, much like his father's. She thought, *He's so grown up; he's already trying to schedule new activities in his life, and he's making life changes.*

"Don't get me wrong, I've enjoyed all the hiking, swimming in the lake, boating, everything, but since I'm in the science institute I'm starting to think I need a change. I already looked into a camp called 'STEM,' meaning science, technology, engineering, and mathematics. It's for premed high school students. Mom, it has everything I would need to study in the medical field."

His long, dark lashes fluttered as he nervously blinked.

"Okay, Cove, tell me more about this camp. I will have to call them and find out about your safety. What is the name of the camp and its location?"

She became serious and a little troubled at the thought of her young son studying the science of medicine at such a young age.

"It's called the Boston Leadership Institute in Wellesley, MA."

His thoughts so wrapped up in going, he sat staring with pleading eyes; his voice cracked as he spoke, and it was all he could say.

"Cove, that's so far away. The furthest you have ever traveled to a camp was the YMCA at Glen Cove. I have to talk this over with your father. In the meantime, I will research this camp."

She researched and found their publication. She thoroughly read the list of academic and career information of the ideas and concepts that drove his curiosity, and now she understood the change he was going through, physically, and his ideas about wanting to save the world. So, she sat at her computer and found the website and began to read.

Boston Leadership Institute Summer Program for premed high school students.

High school students who are considering medicine can explore the health sciences in premed summer programs. The answer for high school students in their science studies and tired of the usual camps could be summer camp with a medical twist. Motivated teenage campers are trading hikes, swimming pools, and meals around a campfire for IVs, sutures, and cervical collars at an innovative medical camp sponsored by Boston Leadership Institute. This program is a premed hands-on experience and insight into medical careers providing hefty incentive for participants, with instruction in skills essential to patient care, such as staring an IV, mixing medications, suturing wounds, and more. This program will be held in the Appalachian Mountain Club. Registration is now!

As she read through the description of the camp's teachings, it gave her a detailed picture of her son's future. She knew this was what he wanted and what he needed.

***

Her motherly thoughts swirled with fears of her son traveling so far at such a young age. Father listened while a web of his own thoughts called to his mind an image of his young son taking on the form of a man.

"We owe thanks to our creator for giving Cove a creative mind. Since he was a child, he had the gift of working with his hands. Do you remember how he carved a bowl out of wood for you? And he used clay to mold a small duck for my desk." He sat hunched over as his mind enjoyed the recollection of the past.

"I know, dear, he is so very clever and has a passion to learn. I think that since he has a scientific mind, we can trust that he will be safe. His curious mind will lead him to where he is supposed to be in his life. I just feel nervous about him being so far away and working with chemicals!"

She pressed her hands in her cheeks and took in a deep breath.

"I think it's time to call Cove into the room and give him the good news that he can go, but he has to listen to our rules about living at this camp." He smiled a reassuring smile at his wife to calm her and show her that all would be well.

"Dad, I heard you call me, what's up?" He sat comfortably in the overstuffed chair and dropped his long legs over the side.

"After much investigation and a phone call to the premed summer camp, we have decided that it is with the best interest for your education to allow you to go."

Before his father could even finish the last word, Cove's eyes lit up with joy as every muscle in his body pushed him into a jump, and with a smile that could brighten any day he ran to his parents. They all hugged, a united hug of appreciation. Cove's hug was a hug of thankfulness.

His father's hug was strong in acceptance. But Mother cradled him like a cherished child, and in that embrace all their worries were set free.

***

The cabins were rustic, all made of round log wood. Each cabin was arranged with four bunkbeds and one single for the counselor. There were three windows with one fan that fit perfectly in one window. The nights were cool in the mountains, so the fan gave a nice breeze through the room. The cafeteria was also the same type of rustic look, with windows all around fitted to wrap around the entire room for a great view of the mountains. It was crowded with about one hundred high school students at the first breakfast time. Cove was able to make friends at his table and found that they were all in the same cabin.

"Hey, my name is Joey. Glad to meet you; I'm premed at my high school. I'm really looking forward to all this science, it's gonna be fun!"

Joey's personality was somewhat like Cove's, energetic yet serious; it was a perfect match.

"Thanks, Joey, for starting up the intro's, I'm Cove, glad to meet all of you. Yeah, this is great! The only thing is it's too bad the bathrooms are outside, in the woods! I just hope I don't find a bear in there."

Cove started a chain of laughter. Their eyes widened with laughter, and there was a signal of feeling safe and comfortable; they all became friends.

It was the next morning after they all attended a group introduction class when they were assigned to take part in their first medical simulation surgery.

"Wow, I didn't think we would start learning surgery so quick!" Cove said with a surprised look on his face, and then a small smile played on his mouth.

The room was still a cabin atmosphere with one surgical bed in the middle of the room.

A human dummy lay on top and covered in a blue gown.

Joey's face turned a pasty white, and he hung his head, wanting to hide his emotions. Then their attention was brought to the teacher standing on the opposite side of the mannequin.

"Okay, kids, I mean ladies and gentlemen, allow me to introduce myself. I am a retired EMS-paramedic. I have done emergency medical care for years and have helped to save many lives. I am also a physician's assistant at our local hospital and have assisted in many surgeries. We just had the opportunity to watch a presentation on surgical procedures. Your faces show signs of fear; not to worry, once we move into this class you will become used to it, and then again you will be able to make your decision if this is the route you want to travel. So, with that said, here is your subject for this morning. Who's my first victim willing to make the first cut? Just as in the video we just watched, I want you to tell me what you find in his stomach."

Then with a smirk the camp counselor extended his hand toward the mannequin on the surgical bed and pointed to its abdomen.

Cove was the first to raise his hand, and he walked to the mannequin. As his eyes examined the dummy, he gave it a quick touch, and he thought, *This is so real. It feels like actual flesh; what did I get myself into?*

His skin color changed to a shade of gray, but he forced himself to continue. He did as he was instructed, hands over abdomen to examine, then placed the scalpel at the proper angle and began the surgical incision. At first glance, Cove would have sworn all he could see were chunks of plastic. He took in a breath and continued.

"I see the small intestine, and I can feel a blockage just like in the video."

Cove was still a little gray as he held the small intestines in his hand, being careful not to shake or let go.

"Good, Cove, so far you are being successful. Finish what you think you should do next. Don't be frightened, this will help you and your classmates know what to expect in the operating room. I think those piano fingers are what helped you."

The counselor smiled with his arms crossed, enjoying his teaching and watching his students, wondering who would be the first to pass out.

Cove's body froze, and his face washed blank as he bent over his first patient to continue the surgery. He succeeded when he removed the blockage of flesh-feeling plastic and held it up for all to see.

There was laughing and applause from all the students.

"Well, I see no one has fainted, so we can move on to the next step. Thank you, Cove, for a well-done first surgery. Who's next?"

Cove was comfortable with his success with his first challenge in his premed class. He felt privileged and in the same way to possess an advantage in learning medical treatments. He knew that surgery was the doorway to a new self—a new self he needed to reach.

***

After a week, he knew he had better make that phone call home to his parents.

"Hi, Mom. I've never been so involved before; this camp is keeping me so busy. There are four levels for me to complete, all different categories. First, it was a week of different types of surgery on a practice dummy. Next, its forensic science, then blood types in the lab and study of anatomy and intubating a patient and so much more. I'm so grateful you sent me."

It was like an explosion in his brain as he poured out all the information and possibilities he shared with his parents.

His mother could feel it through the phone; she knew it was his calling card to a new path for his life.

"Oh Cove, this is great and exciting news. This is a great challenge for you and an adventure for your future. Your father wants the phone now."

His phone call of good news ignited a spark in her heart and a tender smile.

"Hold on, son, don't hang up. Your mom is standing here with tears in her eyes. Tell me more. I could hear some of your conversation with my ear half off the phone." His smile came from deep inside and lit up his eyes as he spoke.

"Well, Dad, I'll also learn how to use staples or sutures, and something I never thought I would like is to study the musculoskeletal and nervous system and how it functions together. I really think I want to learn more of that profession. I think I want to be a neurosurgeon."

He was beaming with contentment. With his positive thoughts, he was focused on his decision, and he was rooted in the thoughts of his new life coming his way.

Living on a North Shore peninsula of Long Island's Nassau County with a small population of twenty thousand, Cove's family was very involved in their town. Glen Cove was their home. He was very comfortable in his small church with its stained-glass windows and tall, white steeple. For most of his teenage years, he was connected to his local church youth group of about twenty teenagers. The pastor was a part of his family. He would often have dinner with them and talk about the upcoming schedule for the teens. The pastor would decorate the church basement with a different theme each Saturday night to bring in the neighborhood teens and keep them busy. One night it was a music theme, where Cove helped his pastor make large music notes out of cardboard and painted them black, then hung them all around the room. A lot of the teens were taking music lessons, so they would bring their instruments and jam. Pastor played the old piano, and their music seemed to blend perfectly. It was there, where they shared in all the activities, that Cove met his lifelong friend, John Frank.

"Hey, there, what instrument did you bring? With those long fingers, it looks like you can play the piano as good as Pastor." John laughed as he pointed to Cove's fingers.

Cove wiggled his fingers back and forth at John. "Ha! No way can I compete with Pastor. But my fingers are pretty good at woodworking. I'm in a woodworking class and have made lots of stuff, like a small jewelry box for my mom and a small, two-bottle wine holder for my dad."

Cove and John had shared their lives since junior high. They were on all the basketball teams, the local baseball league, and in the church ministry. They were best friends, and they considered themselves brothers. But their personalities were opposite. John was extraverted and always reaching out to the other teens. His gestures were always animated, as he talked loudly and was always ready to tell a joke. He was loved by everyone he met.

Cove's personality was more of a serious nature. He was always ready to help in decorating and directing where everything should go for the church events. He was a quality friend. His warmth went right to your core, giving feelings of trust. He listened and made insightful remarks. He made his friends feel like all would be well. That made most of the teens confide in him. Since he was mature for his age, he felt privileged to listen to his friends.

Cove's friends on both the local and church basketball teams demonstrated strong sportsmanship. His team held a strong value of respect toward the opposing team, which they learned from their pastor. When the game was over, even if they didn't score high enough, they all shook hands.

"It's just a game, not our future," Cove would say to his team as he shook each hand.

"Unless you want to be a Michael Jordan." John would comically pretend to bounce the basketball.

Cove loved being involved with his church. He felt like it was his second home. It was where he learned of his creator and how to trust in his pastor's sermons. One sermon in particular really touched his heart during a special youth night.

"My youth team, do you know how amazing you all are and how you have made my dream of teaching teens come true? Watching you develop over the past four years into young ladies and young gentlemen, I am so proud! I am especially grateful to see how your decision-making has brought you into maturity. When you go on after high school, you will encounter a series of decisions, but most of the decisions that will affect your future will be made now. The friends you choose will shape your future, as well as your thoughts of which career you choose and then whom your mate will be. Now open your Bibles to Daniel 1:8–21. Daniel was at a time of crisis in his life. There he was, sitting at the king's table. He was served the king's meat and wine. Daniel had to decide. He learned to say no. Like Daniel, you will face adversities, and you will be able to say no to what will hinder your education and life choices. Will you view your adversities as adventures? Your perspective will make all the difference. You can live in victory! You can be faithful to God. You have learned here in our group everything pertaining to life and godliness. If you rely upon God, He will give you the courage to honor Him. I pray for you that at this year's graduation, you will go forward into a new world better equipped in making the right decisions."

Cove left that night filled with hope for his future and energy to conquer the world.

One Sunday, as he watched his parents pray, he noticed how they held hands while leaning over the pew. It reminded him of when he would walk into the living room and see them holding hands and praying. It was their example of giving, honesty, and dedication to prayer that helped him to find his faith. He knew with his upcoming graduation he had to have faith that he would be accepted to the one college he had applied to that was recognized as the most difficult one to enter for most students because of its low acceptance rate.

One morning just before graduation, Mary came running from the mailbox, shouting with joy and waving a piece of mail high in the air while taking deep breaths to get to the front door. She stood at the bottom of the stairway, calling out to Cove.

"Cove, hurry! Come down here. Look what came in the mail! Looks like a letter of acceptance from Moscow Hospital of Special Surgery. The return address is Moscow, Russia! Oh, Cove, I think you were accepted." She leaned on the edge of the banister, still breathing heavy and holding the mail to her chest.

Cove rushed down the stairs, almost tripping himself; he jumped over the last step and safely landed on his feet. As Mary held the letter with shaky hands, she handed it to Cove. He looked up at his mother and said, "Mom, if this is true, I'll be on my way to the best education in surgery."

He could feel the moisture on his long fingers as he gently opened the letter. Then he read it aloud.

Dear Mr. Robert Ferris: Congratulations! We are delighted to inform you that you have been admitted to one of the finest schools of spinal cord surgeons. Here at Moscow Hospital of Special Surgery, you will embark on our program that will lead you straight to medical knowledge. You will obtain a Bachelor of Science degree and further your education in our medical doctor program.

In recent years, nearly twenty thousand students have applied for the sixteen hundred openings in the freshman class. The admissions committee has taken great care to choose individuals who present extraordinary academic and personal strengths. In voting to offer you admission, the committee has demonstrated its firm belief that you can make important contributions during your college years and beyond.

Our summer program begins August first, where you will receive an invitation for orientation. We have a hospitality unit where you may bring your parents for a two-day seminar introducing you to our facilities and our professors, including the surgeons for your physician-in-training program.

We look forward to having you join our medical team.

Yours sincerely, Dr. Albert Brezukaev.

Tears flowed from Mary's eyes. She smiled up at Cove. Just the sight of him opening up the letter had been enough for her to release the breath that she hadn't realized she had been holding. The momentum of her heartbeat quickened with excitement for him. Yet deep within, there was a little sorrow as she hugged her son. He was leaving behind his childhood. "Well, Cove, I guess we better start calling you Dr. Robert Ferris."

His father came over and joined in the hug.

"Cove, we gave you that nickname, just a little tease, because we live here at Glen Cove. But now the teasing is over. Respectfully, we call you Dr. Ferris."

***

Cove's last days of school were filled with anticipation of that graduation moment. He attended many parties, where his friends shared what colleges had accepted them.

Cove wasn't worried about his future because he was a brilliant young man who excelled in math and science and held the highest academic achievements. Because of his awards of excellence, he was asked to deliver the valedictory speech at his high school graduation. He felt the soft panic as he rose to the podium, and then it suddenly faded as he looked out and saw his parents sitting in the front row.

"I was asked to deliver the valedictorian speech, so I say to you *valedicere* from my Latin studies, farewell. We can reflect on the four years we have spent together at this high school. We learned to vote for our class presidents, a segue into the real life of making choices. Our debate classes taught us how to view and understand one another's opinions. I think of what one of our teachers said to me the other day about how college students are becoming more nontraditional, and that made me think, 'We high school students, through social media, have also become more nontraditional.' Some of us have studied law and have used that study in our mock trials, learning how to prosecute to prove guilt beyond a reasonable doubt, whereas the defense attorneys attempted to create reasonable doubt so that their clients were deemed innocent. I hope I won't need any of you in my future." He chuckled as the audience laughed with him.

"Others, like myself, have worked hard in the early medical field studies of human biology, psychology, and chemistry, hoping to touch lives with the healing art of

72

medicine and surgery. Our art teacher has shown us the technique of transforming our thoughts onto canvas, which will lead some of us to the colorful world of art. We became a family, and this has been our home. I have learned to accept who we are, for we all deserve a chance to prove ourselves in this world. As we leave this home and move forward in a new life, it will be a journey of learning because we are ready. We will face obstacles in order to achieve our dreams. It won't be an easy path, but those obstacles will only help us to stand up and pursue our ideas to achieve our goals.

In closing, I thank every teacher for their strong efforts in helping us to reach our goals. We thank one another for the encouragement we shared in completing each year. In the words of Eleanor Roosevelt, 'The future belongs to those who believe in the beauty of their dreams.' Raise your hand and stand if you are ready to face the future of your dreams!"

With an explosive, booming roar, the students stood up, and their hands flew upward, tossing their graduation caps into the air.

Chapter 6
Stepping-Stones

Heather and Jill had new hairstyles for their graduation, as well as their makeup and nails done for their big moment to receive their diplomas onstage. Their moment of accomplishment had finally arrived. It was time to step out into the world that they had prepared for, and that piece of paper would prove all their diligence over the past six years of study. The celebration was over, and their fellow classmates left the auditorium. They shed the uncomfortable blue graduation robes and handed them to their parents. A new stepping-stone was before them with a ticket to freedom.

Richard kept his arm around Heather, his proud smile reaching ear to ear.

"Okay, girls, since we are about an hour away, we decided to stay over at a really nice hotel. It gives us time to change into comfortable clothes, and we can stay later after our celebration dinner with you then head back home in the morning. We'll meet you at the restaurant at, say, 6 p.m.?"

"Yes, Dad, we want to go see our new apartments and get ready for this evening. I'll see you there."

She held her dad's hand while he kissed her forehead. He whispered, "I love you, Heather. I'm so proud."

Margaret was on the opposite side of the wheelchair, and she squeezed her daughter in her arms as tears rolled down her cheeks. "Heather, you're amazing."

Jillian and Jeff stood not so far away, hugging their own daughter.

"Oh, Jill, you have accomplished so much, and you have achieved more than we could ask for." Jillian smiled and stepped back to look at her adoringly.

"Jill, you are the talk of the town at Rockledge Community. I couldn't help but brag about you to our neighbors on the phone last night. We have memories of our old home back in New Jersey and you being around the house, but that was a long time ago, look at what you have become: a grown-up young lady." Jeff held her for a moment, then let go and rubbed his eyes as if the wind had blown in them. He couldn't speak.

Their reservations were ready at an exclusive restaurant. It was now 6:00 p.m. The table was set in gold-and-white cloth. Their parents set balloons in the center of the table that read *Congratulations*! Margaret made sure to put one sunflower at Heather's place setting, as they all sat at the round table enjoying their dinner. Just before their dinner, Richard stood up to make a toast.

"Jill, Heather, you have both brought much joy to our families. Jill your friendship to Heather has been real devotion. You have accomplished so much in education, here's to new journeys and a new song to be sung. Heather, you have proven that there is no disability, no inability, nothing can stop you from setting goals and achievements.

You have taken life by the storm and you are a role model for the world. God bless you both."

With the clinking of their champagne glasses, they all proudly agreed. The happiness showed in their eyes as they leaned over to give a kiss to their daughters. The waiter served a platter of Cranberry Blue Cheese ball with fruit. Then Jillian and Mary chose an entrée of Lobster with creamy mashed potatoes. The Fathers, Jeff and Joseph chose Filet Mignon with Green Beans. Jill and Heather both enjoyed baked Salmon with wine sauce. When the meal was over, they all agreed on a platter of various mini pastries. Richard and Margaret enjoyed listening to Jillian and Jeff talk about what it was like being an accountant and a real estate broker. And in exchange, the Storm's shared what it was like to be owners of two stores on the Jersey shore, which were both sold when they sold their home and retired to Florida.

"I can't tell you how many times in a week we are asked to donate to a certain cause, which we don't really mind. Living at that time in Point Pleasant, our town assumed we were rich because we had our own business, and two at that. But it's okay. It was for our town and our neighborhood." Margaret softened as she spoke about Point Pleasant.

"Well, Margaret, tell them how we sometimes had to eat our lunch standing up, it got so busy during the summer months in both stores. I'd call or text her and say I couldn't wait to get home and have a sit-down dinner." Richard laughed heartily and sat back in his chair.

Jeff said, "That is interesting and sounds quite busy. For myself, I've always been intrigued by the world of accounting. I made my decision way back in high school. I was so good with math that it was easy for me to become a CPA. Although certain seasons are long, overall, I still tried to make it home to be with my girls, especially to see my little Jill for our family dinners." He reached over to pinch her cheek. "Hey, do you need an accountant?" Jeff tapped Jill's head, laughed, then took a sip of his wine.

Jillian placed her hand on Jeff's shoulder. "Yes, dear, that's true. I have to say he tried very hard to get home earlier than usual a few times during the week. I also tried to schedule my clients for early in the morning when I was taking Jill to school, then made sure my last house showing was done before 6 p.m. Even while she was in college, I still liked getting home early. I guess it's become a routine. Well, that's all in the past now that we live in Florida, but I really do miss the change of seasons." She gave a loving smile to her husband in agreement. They continued their dinner and entertaining conversation in their celebration of both daughters' achievements. Their friendship had formed through their daughters. By sharing their lives through all the graduations and dinners, they had become a family.

***

The next day, Heather and Jill sat at their favorite café just outside of the campus drinking their favorite coffee, reminiscing about the previous day.

"Wow, look at this diploma. University of Marine Sciences, I guess all that chemistry, calculus, and biological discovery that has been swimming in my dreams was well worth it." Heather looked toward Heaven in thankfulness as she pretended to wipe the sweat from her brow.

Jill's smile spread across her face. "Well, now, since we're done with our bachelor's and master's, do you think we should go for a PhD?"

Heather glanced back at her with the slightest curve at her mouth's corner. "Hold on, sister. You're always thinking ahead. Let's just enjoy this year and get ready for our future. We've been accepted to stay on as biologists to continue with our profession, also to teach new students, and live here on the premises. This is our future! What more could we ask for?"

"Oh, Heather, you're always so levelheaded. I think because your personality is so education driven, you'll do great in marine molecular biology."

"I hope so, Sis. My hope is to prevent and cure disease for all of us, both humans and my favorite marine life. Isn't it great living on this campus? And who would have thought that this old wheelchair would have made so many friends? Especially when I introduce myself with Mr. Steel." They laughed a loud belly laugh. Heather gave her wheelchair some loving taps.

Jill leaned forward on the round table, sipping her coffee. "We have made wonderful friends from each class. My marine biology class has this one really nice guy. You know, the one with the sandy-brown hair?"

"Oh yeah? Frank?" Heather asked with humor in her eyes, which summoned a dimple in her cheek.

"Well, we talked the whole year and met up for coffee, but nothing serious. He is so focused on his work and degree he doesn't see past the beakers and chemicals. That's all he talks about, nothing really interesting, I know all about that." Jill's eyes drooped with a hint of sadness. Heather tried to lighten the mood for her.

"That is so funny. Maybe once he's done with his love affair with those beakers, during the graduation break you can ask him out to dinner."

"Yes, Heather, I will. At least I'll try. You know I'm glad our parents decided to retire here in Florida, even though we live on campus and don't live at home with them. They're only forty minutes away. We can see them whenever we are free from our studies since we are more involved here." Jill gave a wave for another refill of coffee.

"Yeah, Jill, Rockledge Community, you know, that retirement village for old people." Heather slowly pushed away from the table, hunched her shoulders in pretending to be old with a cane and laughed.

"Oh yes, we can visit them, but that's when we don't have any house parties to attend."

Jill crinkled her nose and gave Heather a little sly grin. Then Jill gave a silly wink to Heather.

"Well, we are adults now, and the administration has given us such beautiful living arrangements compared with our dorm rooms. But it was good to be in a dorm and have classes but to also be interning with our professors, a hands-on experience. So, it was learning and studies at the same time. It really paid off. Even though my dorm was very tight, with two small windows. Every room was small, and the bathroom was practically almost in the tiny kitchen. But then again, you already had such a private dorm, didn't you!"

"Yeah, just my wheelchair and me! And having everything wheelchair accessible made it so easy to live and study. It was especially made for students with disabilities. It was small, though, just enough kitchen to prepare food and coffee, but I'm not complaining. I appreciate that I had a place to live. Let's go check out our new apartments, and by the way, you're around the corner of the building where my apartment is. I can speed over to you anytime with these race car wheels." Heather made a quick spin in her wheelchair, laughing.

Jill chuckled. "Glad there's enough room between tables for you to do that! Now that the graduation ceremony is over, tomorrow is Monday morning and back to work. I have to continue with the recording of all the data and maintaining records. I forgot to ask you, what you are working on all week that you can't roll over to my end of the building?"

"Well, I've been dissecting microorganisms, like fungi that my professor dropped on my desk yesterday! And the parasites in that vial left in the refrigerator. I better get to work early tomorrow morning." Her worry was plain to see as she held her head, then quickly turned around in her wheelchair and waved a "let's go" to Jill. They headed to their apartments. The memorable day of excitement continued as they entered their new apartments and their future. Heather rode up the ramp to the first floor and into her new place. As she opened the door, she took in a breath of excitement in seeing the apartment was a perfect fit for her. It was furnished with all updated furniture. The living room was so spacious with two large windows, and the curtains were already hung on the rods. *Perfect color blue*, she thought. The sofa had a gold-and-blue pattern that matched perfectly with the window curtains. It was an open concept where the kitchen was part of the living room, which made it easy for her to wheel through. The kitchen counter was low enough for her to reach the sink and especially the coffee pot. The bathroom was specialized to fit a person with disabilities. She sat back and looked around and was so satisfied with everything that would accommodate her.

This is all great, and I have been well taken care of all these years. And despite my disability, I have accomplished my degree, but I still pray that God will make me able to stand up straight on my own someday.

As Jill entered her apartment, she stood amazed at the sight of the one large window that brought so much light into the room. The curtains that draped across the window and softly fell to the carpet were a light blue. All the furniture matched the curtains. The kitchen was small but filled with dishes, cups, and a much-needed coffee pot. Everything was in place for her, and she was so happy to have her own apartment and privacy to continue to study. She sat down on the sofa and looked around in amazement and gratitude to see all that she had received.

This is like a dream. I made it through the first part of my college life. Now I can continue on to the next part. And I'm so glad I'm close to Heather's apartment so I can be there for her when she needs help, even though she's so independent, she chuckled to herself.

***

There was a passion that drove Heather into the life of a molecular biologist. She had a curious mind, so this trait really fit her well. Even though her desk was cluttered with papers and notes of all her works, she always kept a ceramic pot filled with a lavender plant on one side of her desk. It made her feel more at home rather than always having the feeling of being surrounded by machines. The fragrance of the lavender reduced stress for her. Since the other side of her desk sat by a molecular electron microscope, when she felt overwhelmed, she would just look at her plant, inhale the scent, and feel the calmness.

Her desk, which was toward the corner of the room, shared some space with her coworker, Josmary, who was already busy using her traditional electron microscope. Their conversations typically concerned how to advance in their work or their plans for the weekend. She often brought Heather a fresh-brewed coffee, which gave them a moment to stop and just relax.

"Hey, Heather, I noticed you do very well with problem-solving. I watched you working yesterday. You really are moving fast into this field." Josmary sat back and sipped her coffee. She was thrilled to watch and learn from Heather in action. She was an easy-going, laid-back type of person, not so chatty, which Heather liked. Heather felt a little conversation was good to help get through the day, and Josmary was perfect that way.

"Thanks, Josmary. This coffee is really strong. What did you add, a couple of shots to it?" They both laughed. Josmary knew her personality.

"Well, I knew a couple of coffee shots would help us get through the day. Glad you noticed with just one sip! This career is fascinating, challenging, and rewarding. I guess a day in the life of a molecular biologist is fulfilling, don't you think?" Josmary said with a little smirk at the corner of her mouth.

"I guess so. It's unpredictable with all this research, though, I'm thinking in the near future I would like to become more involved with another professional career pathway, like in a scientific institution." She spoke as she continued to study the cytoplasm from the microscope and logged her interpretation of her results of the organelles.

"You know, it's already been two years here at this lab. I sometimes feel like I need to know more. I want to do more. I'll have to look into it." Heather smiled at her coworker, and then they finished up with their work. It was the end of the day, and they began cleaning all the equipment they had used with a special bleach product that the Centers for Disease Control and Prevention recommended. They had just finished wiping down the microscopes and desks when Jill walked in.

"Well, I'm done for the day with all the DNA and RNA. I'm tired and hungry. Let's go out for dinner." She rested her arm on a computer, tapping her fingers and waiting for their answer. "There is a new restaurant downtown. Let's try it."

Heather rolled herself away from her desk and looked at her colleague sitting next to her. Josmary said, "You two go ahead. I'm exhausted. I'm going home." She was amused by Jill's behavior and gave a lighthearted laugh. Heather gave her a high five, and she left. The two girls went ahead to the restaurant and enjoyed a nice dinner. It gave them time to express ideas they had for advancing in their profession.

"You know, Jill, I've been thinking, two years have passed so quickly since getting our degrees. I think it's time to continue our education. At least, I feel I need to move on. Remember what you said the day after graduation about getting a PhD? Well, I've been giving it some strong thought." Heather glanced up at Jill, hoping there was some power in her talk and that she would encourage Jill to agree.

Jill lit up at the idea. "You are absolutely right! I'm in! Let's make an appointment for tomorrow with the school counselor."

***

During the five years of academic study and research that included summer work, they prepared for their dissertations, choosing a research topic and devoting significant time to planning and structuring all the written work. Heather's personality changed from quick and inventive verbal humor to anxious and moody from lack of sleep and constant studies and researching for her dissertation. Once her face was soft with the beginnings of laugh lines. Now it was creased with frown lines. All she could think about was her degree and her work. She became withdrawn, preferring solitude over her studies. Daily after work and on weekends, she would stay at the library, which was offered to all upcoming students and staff from the University of Marine Sciences and held all the most important research information for students and colleagues.

Early one evening, Heather sat in the company's library, thinking, *It's six o'clock, and I'm sitting here with all my books waiting for her. I even took out what she would need to get her started. Where is she?* She felt herself getting annoyed as she rubbed her forehead. She thought, *That girl runs on her own clock!*

Just then, Jill came running in. "I'm sorry, Heather, I was on the phone, setting up a date for this Friday night." She sat with a quick flop into the wooden chair opposite Heather. Heather said with a red face, "You know, in this day of texting, you could have texted me while you were on the phone talking to this whomever. Don't leave me sitting here when I already reserved these books for you."

"Hey, I'm only ten minutes late. Why are you getting so cranky?" Jill was still out of breath from running.

Heather snapped at Jill, "I am here to further my studies. I'm not waiting for you anymore. You can get your own books out on your own time. You're going out on a date Friday night when you should be getting your dissertation started. You're ridiculous!"

"Okay, Heather Study This, Study That. You never get out and enjoy an evening with a date. The work will get done, just stop getting so bossy. You've changed. All you do is work and research, study here, then go home and study again. I'm ridiculous? Look at yourself throwing a hissy fit! You've become a hermit. I'm tired of your bitterness."

Jill then grabbed her books and left in a huff. She thought, *I could engage in battle with her right now, but what would be the point? She's been so irritable; I'll just leave it alone.*

A week had passed, and Heather and Jill did not talk. There was something about the largeness of the university. It gave space in its accommodation to various studies. Jill's office was not far from the science lab, where she would always walk over talk for a few minutes, but that ended now. Heather would always call Jill and they would leave together to go back to their apartments, but Heather traveled alone now.

Jill felt gloomy sitting in her apartment. Every shade of feelings swept over her as she thought of all the years they had spent together in a sisterly friendship. She couldn't believe that Heather would not reach out to her and make amends. She thought, *I have to reach out to her since she's being so stubborn.*

Sitting in her apartment, Heather looked around and felt her home was sunless in spite of the large windows. She knew it was because Jill wasn't in her life any longer. She thought, *She believed in me in a way no one else ever had and no one else will. I feel like I betrayed her. I feel guilty about the way I spoke and ended this friendship; it's like ice in my stomach. I know I have a strong personality, but Jill always seems to balance me.*

Jill was always the patient one in the friendship. She thought back to junior high and high school and remembered how Heather would always have a snappy answer and they would laugh about it. She kept pacing the living room, back and forth, back and forth. Finally, she couldn't stand the silence between them any longer, so she decided it was time to end this nonsense of not speaking to each other. She went to the nearby flower shop and picked up one sunflower.

Heather was thinking about her moodiness. She knew this wasn't normal for her character. She thought, *Feeling moody is my cue to get out of this cocoon and get in touch with my reflective moments. This isn't in me. I have always found myself in control. I realize why I am so irritable; I allowed my studies to overtake me, and I need to make better choices. I need to call Jill.*

At that moment, the doorbell rang. When Heather opened the door, it was Jill. Heather burst into tears and begged for forgiveness. They sat together and both cried.

The conflict had cut deep, but they realized that their friendship was so important that the bond they had was incredibly strong. They both learned about forgiveness. Time healed their wounds. And time brought them again a year later to graduation, this time with PhDs in cytogenetics where both loved the study of chromosomes and DNA cells.

***

The graduation ceremony was over, both sets of parents exchanged cameras for the excitement of photos with their daughters. They went to their favorite restaurant and were seated by a window with a view of a garden filled with petunias, salvia, marigolds, geraniums, and Heather's favorite, sunflowers.

Richard put his arm around Heather and said, "I want to make a toast for my two favorite girls. This is a momentous occasion to watch you both reach your goals. With your PhDs now accomplished, we can call you doctor. My, Heather, you have risen to become a voice for so many who struggle with a physical challenge. You have led the way for so many to reach their goals and find strength in their identity as a woman."

He turned to his daughter with joyful tears. Margaret, who was also sitting next to her, felt a strong sensation in her throat and wasn't able to speak.

Jill's parents agreed with a clinking of glasses. Jeff was also touched.

"I also am so very proud of our girls. The both of you have made a positive difference in this world." He swallowed hard, holding back emotions. "Little girls grow up so fast and then become women but are always part of their families and always part of a father's heart. Here's to a new life, new experiences, and the changes about to happen for you. It is also important to us all that you find romance and your one true love." Jeff wasn't ashamed of the tears that fell on his cheeks.

The evening ended, and their parents headed home with a deep feeling of satisfaction, knowing they had raised their daughters with life's important teachings so they could achieve their goals with the gifts and talents God had given them.

Jill asked, "Well, now, sister, we graduated together with our bachelor's and master's degrees, and now a PhD. What more could we ask for? What an amazing life. I never thought I would reach this far."

Heather spent a moment in pensive silence as she reflected back to her past experiences with her studies and school.

Jill lit up with a burst of energy like a lively child. "Yes, just fathom the mysteries of God, how He guided us to this part of our lives. I'm excited to see where we will be next. Who knows, maybe we'll travel across the world."

Heather turned to Jill, close to tears. "I like what your father said at his toast to us, that we will find romance and our one true love. I hope it was also a prayer because in this wheelchair it will be hard to find someone to love me."

"Hey, come on now, this is not the time to feel so pouty. Just believe and pray. You've already gone on a few dates; they just weren't the right ones. Please believe me. I feel love in the air. It's going to happen." Jill then gave Heather a warm smile and a strong hug.

Chapter 7
Mr. Steel

Eleven years of college had passed. Heather, who was now twenty-eight years old, felt deep pleasure and satisfaction in her own achievements. She had worked at this laboratory throughout her years at the university and knew each step that had to be taken with precaution. She often worked quietly at her lab desk, preparing biological specimens for chromosome testing. She was researching inheritable traits, harvesting, examining, and analyzing chromosomes for abnormalities and using the best equipment in microscopes and computerized equipment to carry out her testing. Then she stopped and remembered her first class at the University of Marine Sciences.

I can't believe I'm using the best equipment. I never thought I would come this far. At first, it was a dream, but it's as real as day. I've gone from using the microscope with the changing magnification measuring the distance between the lenses to this modern, digitally enhanced microscope, which is more sensitive to the eye. I can complete so much more testing so quickly. I wonder if there will ever be an advancement in science for my spine? Then she leaned on her desk and held her head, thinking, wishing, and hoping.

A few weeks passed, and on this one particular day, as Jill and Heather were on their way to the lab, they noticed a new posting for job offers in New York City on the university announcement board. It was a posting from a private institution named the New York Microbiology Laboratory for the position of cytogeneticist needed. Heather was thrilled to see that her credentials met the requirements for certification and licensure in the states of New York and Florida.

After carefully reading the posting, there was a spark of wonder in Heather. Then she rubbed her hands together as if holding a secret and quickly went into her bag and took out a pad and pen and began writing down the information. She felt a strong connection to this company since her credentials met the requirements for all three levels of genetics analysis. She would be able to utilize her studies on genetic testing, biochemical and molecular methodologies.

Jill also began writing down the information. When she finished, she stretched her arms open wide and took in a breath.

"This is amazing! My dad said in his toast that there will be a change! This must be it. Here we go, Heather. Get ready for another change!"

Heather rocked in her wheelchair with her arms waving, and Jill danced around in a circle. It was like they were having a party.

They gave the notice a once-over one more time to make sure they had read it correctly and decided to call at the end of the day. They submitted their resumes for review and waited for a response. Within a week, they were invited to come in for an interview. Heather received the first phone call, and the date was set for the following month. Her excited breathing was so strong it could blow away leaves. Heather quickly called Jill with the exciting news.

"Jill, wow! This is unbelievable. I have all the credentials and more! I'm scheduled for an interview!" Her eyes gleamed, and her voice went into a high pitch.

On the other end of the phone, Jill responded, "Well, here we go again on another one of your adventures, Heather. I also have an appointment for an interview." Her eyes sparkled as she slightly raised an eyebrow.

"There comes a time when change is good, Jill. We can't stay set in one way. It's time to move on. I just can't believe that we were both accepted for interviews so quickly for two new positions in New York! Even though we'll be leaving behind our parents in Florida, maybe after a while, I bet they'll move to New York. Now I'm glad they never sold the cottage at the Jersey shore."

"Yes, you're right. We can go to the beach and sleep at the cottage. It can be an escape from the big city!" She gave a smile like the Cheshire cat, grinning from ear to ear.

"You're right. It will be a fresh start for all of us. One page finished and another to begin. We'll convince them to move once we get settled."

Within a month, they were in New York for their interviews. They booked a hotel for a few days since their interviews were set a couple of days apart. Heather was nervous being in the big city; she felt it was so different from living in Florida. She was ready, and the next morning she arrived at the office for her interview. She nervously sat across from the interviewer and hoped that sitting in her wheelchair and not the office chair would not cause a reason not to be hired. But rather the person who sat behind the desk spoke directly to her and maintained eye contact throughout the conversations. After an hour of questions, she was hired.

A couple of days later, Jill found herself in the same office. After she explained her knowledge of cytogenetics and recording data and identifying data for each sample, she explained how she would submit both specimens and accompanying information for coordination sites. With a strong handshake from the interviewer, Jill left feeling she had achieved her goal to be hired. She was to begin her new experience in a month.

It was a bittersweet moment as they left their first professional home at the university, a sadness in leaving a place of strong friendships and fond memories. All their colleagues brought them together one night for a farewell dinner. There was dinner and drinks. One of the colleagues, Nicky, made a special toast to their departure.

"Girls, what a pleasure it has been to work with you. Congratulations on your well-deserved success, and with the warmth of my heart, we all send you the best wishes for your new adventure. We all love you and will greatly miss you." Then, in a humorous way, he added, "Especially those car rides with Heather!"

Jill thought, *This was my home away from home. I will truly miss them all and my work here, but I feel so confident in moving on to my new location and a new profession.*

***

The airport was noisy. The sound of announcements blared through the terminal. People rushed with their luggage. Lines were long at the weigh-in station as travelers stood holding their tickets. But the sounds didn't drown out Heather's and Jill's conversations with their parents as they moved through the airport. They stopped for hot pretzels and coffee, and when they passed the ice cream station, they couldn't resist.

When they reached the check-in for their flight, Jeff helped them with their luggage at the weigh station. Once they reached the boarding gate, he gave them their tickets. Both mothers started to cry, then Jillian took both of their hands.

"Girls, we have all been through many changes together: we followed you to Florida, took delight in watching your graduations, and now we celebrate your new pathway to another new life in New York. It's hard for moms to see their only children leave. But you're not just leaving, you are expanding your dreams and have become successful. We are so very proud." Margaret and Jillian took turns and kissed them on their foreheads and squeezed their hands. Richard coughed, clearing his throat, and turned to them.

"I have one message for you both. The two most powerful words I can say right now are 'I believe.' I believe in you, and I believe we will be together soon. Our love is the bridge to our connection." Teary-eyed, his held his daughter, kissed her forehead, and stepped back.

Margaret grabbed Heather's hands and whispered in her daughter's ear, "I love you so much, don't be surprised if we show up at your door with a new mortgage payment." With a wink, she turned away, dabbing her eyes.

***

Heather adapted very quickly to her new surroundings in New York City. Her apartment was much larger than the one in Florida, but with the same accessories for disabilities. The sun reflected through the large window in her living room, giving her ample light in the morning. She enjoyed the view of the Hudson River, which she thought of as her backyard facing the west side of Manhattan. She could see a little café at the end of the street and thought, *I'll call Jill. We have to meet there for a bite to eat. This is so exciting.*

Jill was close to Heather's building. She was amazed at the contemporary design of her apartment. She was happy that it was already fully furnished with matching contemporary furniture. She sat on the sofa and enjoyed the huge window where she could see all the Manhattan buildings that she had read about. There was a magazine next to her, so she began to read about Manhattan-style living. There were names of famous actors who lived right in the Upper West Side. She called Heather to tell her what she had just read in the magazine.

"You're not going to believe who lives in this area: Steve Martin, Amy Schumer, and Jerry Seinfeld! We're as famous as them!"

They both laughed a good belly laugh. They were both excited and a little nervous, but having a doorman and elevator operator made them feel very safe and secure. Each morning in Heather's building, the operator would reach her floor and greet her by tipping his hat.

"Good morning, Heather. Today will be a good day," he would say as he tipped his hat and gave a warm, polite smile.

"Thanks, Mr. Bates. You always send a positive feeling my way. Were you always in this building?"

"I have been here for the past ten years. Before that, I worked on Wall Street for thirty years. This is considered my retirement. I was the vice president of the Nationwide Accounts Incorporated. It's closed down now." He had the kind of smile that made her feel happy. "I've raised my family, and now I'm waiting to be a grandfather. Then I will really retire, but until then, I'm here to help. Well, here you are. Go straight ahead to Mr. Santos. He'll get the door for you."

Mr. Santos was another gentleman. He also tipped his hat, then held the door open for her. He would always speak Spanish to her. In the morning, he said, "Buenos días," and in the evening, he would say, "Buenas noches."

As she left, she thought, *Mr. Bates is very polite and interesting. I can see his age by the small amount of gray hair that escaped from under his cap. I'd like to hear some of those Wall Street stories, and he looks at me so gently. I guess he is the definition of a gentleman. And I love Mr. Santos' accent. He gives a flair to his words.*

Jill was in hurry. She felt like the elevator in her building would never get to her floor. *I know Heather is waiting for me downstairs. I wish this man would hurry.*

Mr. Oliver, the elevator operator, greeted her. "Good morning, Miss Jill. You seem a little untidy this morning. Is everything alright?"

He stepped aside to let her enter, then started the elevator to go down.

She fixed her jacket and pulled back her hair. "Oh, I'm sorry, I didn't realize I was so easy to read. Yes, I'm a little late."

"It's okay, Miss Jill. You will get there on time. Seems like we are all in a rush these days when actually we will get to where we are going. It just takes some time." He spoke with a slight accent.

She enjoyed listening to him. "I like your accent. Where are you from?"

"I came here thirty years ago from England–Liverpool, that is. I was twenty at the time with big dreams." He remained focused on the lighted numbers going down.

"Did you find your dream, Mr. Oliver?" Jill was still fixing her hair.

"My father was an iron worker, and so I followed him as soon as I graduated high school. When he passed away, my mom and I came to this country where I also stayed with my trade for over thirty years. After all that time, I had enough of that hard labor and found this and have been here for over ten years. Well, Miss Jill, here is your stop. See you this evening. Cheerio."

As Jill ran to the entrance, the doorman, Mr. Jones, tipped his hat and said, "Rise and shine, Jill, it's another good day."

She smiled at him and ran outside looking for Heather. She thought, *Mr. Oliver's accent is such a playful tune, like an actor. I could listen all day. And I just love the early morning greeting from Mr. Jones. This is great!*

At her new position, Heather worked diligently as she placed a round of vials in the centrifuge. Covered in a protective mask with goggles and gloves to ensure her safety, she carefully collected samples of fluids and tissue for chemical analyses. She was so busy calibrating and preparing solutions that she didn't hear the group of young students enter the laboratory. Her eyes were keenly examining tissue through the microscope when she heard a voice interrupt her concentration.

The clinical microbiology lab director stood with her clipboard and eight new students, trying to get Heather's attention. "Heather, Heather...excuse me, Dr. Storm!" Her forceful voice increased each time she said her name.

Heather looked up and realized her director was speaking to her.

"Oh, Dr. Harris, I apologize. I wasn't aware that anyone had walked into the room," she replied, lifting her eyes from the microscope with a flushed face. Then she noticed the students standing next to Dr. Harris, holding notebooks and staring at her.

"Dr. Storm is our top cytogeneticist. She will show you what is required of your classes and hands-on experiments during your first course. Watch and listen because you will be tested later." She introduced each one to Heather. Then, like a flash of light, she was gone, leaving behind eight frightened students.

Heather remembered that feeling of being a new student, so with understanding, she said, "Allow me to introduce you to my most trusted associate. His name is Mr.

Steel, and he goes wherever I go. I just want to get that out of the way so you focus on me and not the wheelchair." Although her words were firm, she was still humorous to help dislodge the serious looks on their faces. "We are all here for one purpose: to help find cures with our advances in science. Our future discoveries will be for humans, and animals as well, and will result in someone leaving the prison of a sickness. We will offer relief to their pain."

The tension broke, and all were able to adopt a more lighthearted attitude on their performance while in the lab. As the days passed, she befriended and formed a healthy, informative relationship with the students. They all worked hard under her expertise and learned to trust her.

Chapter 8
Wearing the White Coat

It was a chilly morning for Cove as his hand glided over the mist on the inside of his window. His residency in Moscow had made arrangements for their interns to accommodate them with furnished apartments near the hospital during their time in their studies in their practice. As he looked up and watched the dark clouds circling above, he remembered a day long ago on a beach and a little auburn-haired girl. He stopped for a moment and went into his closet where he had stored away a memory from that day. He took down the tiny box and lifted out a half shell. He remembered how he had held it tightly as he kept his eyes on the beach as his father drove away. He held it to his ear and heard the sound of the ocean. Then there was the sweet scent of the beach. He pictured how he had held it so tightly, hoping to see her as he left.

It's been four years since I arrived in Moscow. Why in the world have I kept this all these years? I can still see her emerald eyes looking into mine; seems like she enters my thoughts every once in a while, he thought. Then a voice interrupted his memories.

"Hey, Cove—sorry, I mean, Dr. Robert Ferris. Let's go, this is our most important day!" shouted his friend Dr. John Frank as he opened Cove's front door and leaned halfway in.

Cove slowly closed the box and placed it back on the shelf, then hurried to the front door. His face was still flushed from his thoughts of the shell and the little girl.

"Okay, here I am. I'm ready. I can't believe we have finished our intern then residency and we are done with our fellowship. Wow, it's exciting to know that we are now attending physicians. It has been an honor to study and assist directly with Dr. Brezukaev, the neurosurgeon laureate of the Russian physicians. What an opportunity!"

Cove rushed to find his keys again, while his heart was overflowing with excitement and joy.

"Yes, and he also won the award for inventing a special way to heal patients with the most complicated injuries. And now we'll be joining him in all his surgeries." John then collapsed on the nearby overstuffed recliner. He stretched his legs over the side and with a loud yawn said, "Hurry up, guy, I need more coffee!"

"Yeah, just think: in the past four years, we assisted him as medical students. It has been the best time in my life. Well, let's get on with it, then. There's less traffic now that the tourists have left. And much quieter. So, let's go get that coffee." Cove jiggled his keys as a signal to John, and they ran out the door.

***

Cove couldn't find anything that made him happier than being in the operating room assisting Dr. Brezukaev, who was the chief surgeon. He learned the importance of how to calm a patient before the surgery and explain the procedure once again. He also made sure to visit his patients after surgery to make sure they were comfortable and check on their vitals. He felt proud to identify the problem with the chief doctor and then fix it and watch their patient return home.

This one particular morning as he roamed the hallways making his rounds with John, the junior resident stopped him.

"Hey, Dr. Ferris, I've been looking for you. The first case today is yours. Dr. Brezukaev will supervise your surgery. Get ready in the scrub room at 9 a.m. You will be performing a laminectomy on this patient. Not so hard, right?"

Cove was floored. He felt a heaviness in his chest. He turned to his friend with a flushed face. "John, did you hear that? I'm doing my first surgery alone!"

"Hey, it's okay. You'll be calling the shots, but you're not alone. I'll be in there, and most importantly, Dr. Brezukaev will be supervising. Don't worry. This is your big break to prove your skill. Come on, let's go get ready!"

***

It wasn't the first time Cove had entered the surgical room. This time, he felt a sudden surge of anxiety mixed with heightened excitement. The windowless room seemed more spacious. He moved slowly to his patient, then greeted

Dr. Brezukaev. The doctor stood tall and rigid like a sergeant major. He was a dignified man, sensitive yet direct and forthright in all his remarks. Cove thought of him as if he were leading his residents like soldiers in training.

"Well, my young doctor, are you ready for the first cut?" Dr. Brezukaev's smile was hidden behind his mask, but his eyes revealed an encouraging acknowledgment of all of Cove's work.

"Yes, Doctor. Thank you." The filtered air with the scent of anesthesia and medications filled the room. Cove turned to the head surgery nurse. "Let's begin. Scalpel, please."

The room became serious, with each surgeon watching and assisting. The circulating nurse ran back and forth, obtaining supplies and ensuring the operation remained sterile. The scrub nurse was actively engaged with Cove while handing him each instrument he requested. The anesthesiologist monitored the breathing, heart rate, and blood pressure. Cove carefully removed the bony roof covering the spinal cord to create more space for the nerves to move freely. He removed part of the vertebra that was putting pressure on the nerves of the spinal canal, which he believed was the cause of the patient's chronic pain. All went smoothly in the five hours of Cove's first surgery.

As they left the surgery room and walked into the hallway, Dr. Brezukaev spoke to Cove.

"Dr. Ferris, you did incredibly well for your first unassisted surgery. I will consider you for the next surgery, which will be a little more intense. I am proud of your calmness and expertise. I must say you have improved the quality of life for this patient, and by the way, you can shorten your greeting to me now. Just call me Dr. B."

That was the first time Cove saw Dr. B's smile change from a professional one to a warmer smile. His eyes were steady on Cove as he stood tall with his arms folded, his smile stretched wide across his face. Cove was surprised, and he thought, *He appears more human now.*

"Thank you, Dr. B. I feel I learned so much from today's surgery. From the first incision to the final suture, I gained an unbelievable amount of experience. I learned from you, the best mentor any future doctor could have. But you know, I felt the duration of the surgery lasted a little longer than I had planned. It took a strong mental effort to be precise, but as time moved on, we successfully finished."

"Well done, Dr. Ferris." He leaned closer and gave an encouraging tap on Cove's shoulder. Then, with a quick smile and a nod, Dr. B. quickly walked on to his next patient.

It was the next morning. Cove lay in bed with his mind repeatedly coming back to the prior day's events. It was his day off, *A day of relaxation*, he thought. He jumped out of his bed, peeling away the bedsheets. As he poured his morning cup of coffee, he heard the beeping sound of his cell phone. In the disheveled bed sheets and found his phone.

"Hey, there, Dr. John Frank," Cove said with a sly laugh. "Why are you calling me so early? I was just pouring my first cup of coffee," he said while still trying to take a sip.

"I found a beach not too far from here and visited it last week. Do you believe it? There's a beach outside of

Moscow. A couple of the physician assistants are off, so we thought we would all take the ride together and check it out. You game?" John tapped his fingers, waiting for an answer.

"Sure, why not? Let me finish my breakfast at least."

Cove quickly got ready. After a short time, he could hear the loud sound of John's car horn.

Cove said in a huff as he jumped in the front seat, "Okay, everyone, what's the name of this beach, and how far is it?"

"It's called Podrezovo Beach, and it's maybe about thirty minutes from here. It's worth the ride. I've been there, and the sand is great, and the ocean water is clean. Trust me on this," one of the interns commented from the back seat.

Cove snickered, "Well, this whole time we have been in training with surgeries, we finally get to visit the beach. I almost thought there wasn't one."

"Did you forget we did take a twenty-four-hour break last week to visit the Trinity Lavra of St. Sergius, one of the largest Orthodox monasteries in the world?" John reminded Cove of their window of finding local attractions.

"Yes, I certainly remember that. Especially the cafés serving the homemade bread, pastries, and their special kvass—you know, that soft drink made with fermented bread. I really enjoyed the different taste it had. It wasn't like our sodas back home." As Cove spoke, a vision of his home came to mind, making him a little sad and miss his parents.

Thirty minutes passed, and when they smelled the scent of the ocean, they knew they had found their destination. It was crowded with people sunbathing on beach blankets. They watched as children laughed loudly and ran in between the blankets, kicking up sand. Finding a spot closer to the ocean, they could feel a soft breeze. While they set up their blankets to enjoy some sunbathing, they could feel the hot sand between their toes. They dove into the water, which felt refreshing, and swam awhile, then came back to their blankets to dry off. After a couple of hours, it became late in the hot afternoon, and most of the tourists started packing up and leaving to get ready for the evening dinner and more sightseeing.

It was a restful time for Cove as his mind kept circling back to his own hometown and the beach his family would often visit during the summer. The umbrella his father would always set up for his mom. The different flavors of ice cream he would enjoy while sitting on the beach blanket. The sound of the waves that would soothe him into an afternoon nap he needed after all the running around on the sand.

After a couple of hours of rest on his blanket, his thoughts were interrupted by Louie, an intern.

"Hey, guys, we have been roasting here long enough. I'm seeing mirages of water and food. I'm hungry now. Let's take a walk to the restaurant. Seems like some folks here are heading in that direction. We can have a nice fish dinner." Louie pointed toward the restaurant.

Cove thought, *This guy is always hungry. He's like a hungry bull.*

John looked up and, at the thought of dinner, started rubbing his belly and making hunger sounds. "You're right. I can smell food. My nose wants to follow the aroma. Let's go."

Cove was still in the mood to reminisce about his family and home in Glen Cove, and he decided to walk down to the shore. He said, "Sounds good. I'll catch up with you in a minute. Go ahead and save me a seat."

As he picked himself up, he knelt on one knee and scooped up a handful of sand. He could feel the soft grains slide between his fingers. As he watched it funnel through, his thoughts turned to that one particular summer at the beach. The white sand and the scent of the ocean and the little green-eyed girl he couldn't seem to remove from his memory.

He walked closer to the shoreline and found seashells. Picking up a few and comparing them, he felt none could match the one he had shared with her that day. He thought, *In all my daydreams, I'm back at the beach, the days of innocence and being unaware of the future. Oh, how I wish I could return to that beach, to that time in my life and meeting Heather. Whatever happened to her?*

Chapter 9
A Change in the Air

A couple of years had passed, and Heather's training of the new students ended. She hoped she had instructed them well for their next step in their education. Heather worked with enthusiasm as her tapered fingers, like the fingers of an artist, moved smoothly while conducting the most delicate and complicated experiments. Science was her world, her form of art.

Because she was so absorbed in her work, she couldn't hear a voice echoing in the room. Startled, she froze, then realized it was Dr. Harris.

"Oh, Dr. Harris, I'm so sorry I didn't hear you at first." Heather's face shone a little pink as she looked up.

"I know, Heather, this seems to be a pattern with us," Dr. Harris said jokingly. She quietly kept a protective eye on Heather. She thought of her as a daughter but kept that to herself. She liked her strong personality and especially her carefree way of always greeting people. Heather's comic, upbeat humor always helped others lose sight of her wheelchair. Her display of emotional strength had overcome her disability, and her kindly laughter touched those who came into contact with her.

"I've been thinking, you have been working in this lab for a couple of years now without asking for a break. So, since the weather is so nice and warm, I would like you to take a week or two of vacation. You really need to get out in the sun. I see you becoming paler while working in this lab day and night."

"You're probably right. I do feel tired and could use some natural light!" Heather pointed up to the skylight in the ceiling.

"By the way, I'll also talk to Jill. She seems to be over her head in researching also." She knew that Jill would say yes and that, as close friends, they liked to share their plans and their double dates or meeting up with colleagues for dinner and drinks. "I'll present the same idea to her. Just let me know what weeks you will be going. One of the new interns you have trained can fill in." Dr. Harris made a quick turn and left, heading toward Jill's research room.

***

Jill and Heather talked it over and decided since Heather's parents still owned the beach house it would give them a chance for a free getaway at the beach.

"I've been thinking, maybe my parents' beach house is a good idea. It's been vacant, and it would cost us nothing." Heather imagined the cottage again as she waited for Jill's response.

"Yes! That sounds perfect. A week in the sun. I'd love it," Jill said with a childlike excitement in her voice.

The following week, Jill joined Heather on their road trip to the beach. Heather would always recall when her family vacationed each summer. Her parents would tell her stories of when she was just a baby and they started taking her to this very special cottage at this particular beach. They had rented the same cottage for weeks at a time until they finally bought it. She could remember when she was three years old, sitting under their umbrella and playing in the sand. The white bonnet her mom had her wear to shield the bright, hot sun from her head and face. The little red beach bucket she filled with sand with the yellow shovel. One of her great memories was the vanilla ice cream her dad would give her. She smiled as she remembered it dripping down her chin from the heat of the sun and trying to lick it off. She could still see him laughing as he wiped her chin.

Heather said, "It looks the same. All this time, the cottage hasn't changed. It's been a long time since I've been here. I was only ten years old when we stopped going." She then felt a little misty-eyed about that particular memory of the accident. "I remember all the seagulls in the backyard because I would sit there and throw pieces of bread up into the air so they could catch them. It was fun!" Heather's eyes gleamed at the sight of her old summer cottage. "I'm glad my parents kept it, even though no one stays here. But someone must have painted the shutters. It's such a clean white, and they watered the rhododendron bush. Look at the bright-purple color, and it's so full. I'm glad to see Mom's sunflowers looking so healthy."

"You must have a lot of great memories here. I wish I'd had a childhood like this! But I shouldn't complain. I had a great diving pool in the backyard and lots of parties. Well, this has been an enjoyable time of recollection, but I don't want to waste another minute. Let's get going now. We can clean up later. Come on, let's head to the boardwalk. There's so much to do!" Jill spoke with great enthusiasm.

Heather was used to the roads, but since it had been so long since she had been at the beach house, she made a wrong turn, even though it was only a couple of blocks from the beach. She wanted to drive there and not use her wheelchair. Finally, they were back on track and arrived at the beach entrance.

Jill walked alongside of Heather's wheelchair, thinking to herself, *how will I be able to help her through the sand dunes just so she can look again at a place her memory keeps repeating? Doesn't she realize that this is in the past, never to be relived again? But I just want to make her happy, so I will not express what I really feel. Memories are eternal, I guess.*

Heather was able to move steadily with her new, motorized wheelchair. She was challenged by the steep slope and going through the narrow bridge that led her to the sand. She didn't go too far ahead, just a little off the ramp, and she stopped to look out at the ocean. She remembered how she had tried to reach that little bridge when she had heard a loud shriek and darkness had overcome her as she had heard her father's voice calling her and fading.

She faced a vast stretch of sand with the gentlest hue of gold. A breeze brought the scent of the ocean waves as she watched the hustle and bustle of families and groups of children running and playing. She remembered the tiny bungalows on the side of the beach. The colors of the parasols brought back the memory of her meeting the little boy with large, deep-brown eyes and his long fingers trying to open the shell. She laughed at the thought of how they had run down to the shore and back and how strong her little legs were and how fast she could run. She thought to herself, *His name was Cove. And he didn't know why he had that name.* Then she gave a little smile. *I remember how he gave me the other half of the shell; it was such a magical moment that has remained in my heart. I sometimes wonder why.* She spoke while staring out at the ocean without a blink.

"Jill, I wish I could just walk down to the ocean and pick up the sand and shells like a child again. My life was so happy, so simple."

Jill quickly turned to face Heather with her mouth and eyes opened wide. She thought, *She never cries, she never complains, she never talks about the past. Only twice has she ever cried and talked about the accident. Once when we were on the boardwalk in Florida looking for ice cream, she talked briefly about it. Another time when she got home from our double date, she called me and mentioned she wouldn't be in a wheelchair if that hit and run didn't happen. I should not have brought her here!*

"Heather, I've never heard you talk like that. Are you okay? I think we should go. This is too emotional for you. Let's go!" Jill then grabbed the handles of the wheelchair.

"You don't understand. It was almost supernatural. It was such a long time ago. I should have my brain decode these ancient thoughts; don't you think? But you're right, let's just go." Her laughter was a signal of feeling safe while masking that memory and her true emotions.

After they put away all their luggage and cleaned up the place a little, they were ready to venture out for the evening. They went on the boardwalk and found the best ice cream.

Heather stopped to play the water guns, which were easy for her to use. She was happy to see she had won and was able to pick from the first row of prizes. She picked a stuffed dolphin.

"Ha, Heather, out of all the stuffed animals here, of course you would pick a marine animal!" Jill shook her head and laughed. She took a try at the balloon bust with her strong arm and won a prize. "I can pick from the second row, so no animals for me. I'll take that colorful clown."

With Jill hugging her clown and Heather squeezing her dolphin, they continued along the boardwalk. There was an Adventure Aquarium with lots of great exhibits. They went through a dark cove entrance and saw the bat exhibit. Then Jill spotted a huge water tank. "Oh look, up ahead— penguins! I just love them! Let's go!"

They were both amused watching them swim around. Then they moved on to the dolphins. Heather shook her stuffed toy at them, but they just continued to swim around and play.

"Hey, Jill, there's the souvenir store. Let's buy some things."

They wandered through the store and picked up key chains, candy, and even a puzzle with a picture of aquatic animals.

"Wow, a one-thousand-piece puzzle. That will keep us busy while we stay here," Heather said, laughing.

At the end of each day, they found great restaurants for the evening. One in particular was with the ocean view, which blended with the coastal flavors of seafood. This ended up becoming their favorite.

Heather checked the restaurant's sign and made heart signs with her hands.

"Hey, Jill, I think this is the restaurant my mom and dad went to when they were dating. They told me their romantic story where they would meet to have dinner on the boardwalk facing the ocean. And it's at this place that Dad gave her engagement ring. Seems like the name has changed since it's been like thirty years."

"Well, this could be it since their novelty store isn't so far from here. We should have asked your parents before we left. But it's a great romantic story." Jill cupped her chin while her eyes roamed the boardwalk.

"Thanks, Jill, for taking vacation with me. Maybe someday you will have a husband, and you can use my cottage for a weekend away." She looked up at Jill with her sad eyes, which seemed to foretell the coming of both their futures.

"Hey, come on now, you know we'll both find our husbands and come here and share your beautiful cottage. Things will change in our lives—yes, this is true—but our friendship will never change." Jill tried her hardest to cheer up Heather, but in her heart, she also wondered if Heather, with her situation, would ever meet the right man to love and care for her.

A week of fun and relaxation passed quickly. With all the enjoyment at the beach and the boardwalk, they felt well rested. It was also a time of collecting their thoughts. The night before they left, they sat back on the old but comfortable sofas, reminiscing about their high school days. Heather felt so relaxed, as if she were resting beside a brook. Her thoughts spun around, then a brief smile stretched across her face as she began to share her innermost feelings.

"One moment, I was a little girl running with the ground under my feet. Then the bicycle wheels became my feet as I pushed my strong ballerina legs against the pedals. It could have been a bicycle that I could still ride. Instead, it's this. I guess I'm just holding on to my pointless feelings as I look back on my life. I think all these memories are returning because as I look around this untouched house, they all remain. Seeing the same window curtains and the furniture in the same spot, it's like waking up from the longest dream. Most of all it's the memory of the beach, the ocean aroma brought back the best memory of all, the boy on the beach and a shell." She felt a tightening in her throat.

"It's a little tight in here, though. We have to open it up a little so I can ride my wheels through the rooms." Heather nervously rubbed the top of one silvery wheel.

"It's okay, Heather. Don't forget, we have been running around all week here at your favorite place. This house has triggered a rush of memories for you. It's normal to have those feelings. Tomorrow after breakfast, we'll be on our way home and back to work. You know, Heather, our life is like a clock ticking through time, and each day is measured with our own private clock. With all this time passing in your life, you have developed so much knowledge. Even in your wheelchair, you have accomplished what most people could not have mastered," Jill said with a look of concern on her face for Heather, hoping her advice would help.

"You're right, Jill, I never thought of life being measured in time. I see now that time is on my side, or I wouldn't have come this far. Thank you for always being there for me and being such a true friend. I'm feeling a little tired now. I think I'll turn in. It's getting late. But I have to say, I do feel like a transition is going to take place. I don't know why, but I feel good in a sense, like all this was for a reason. So, take that nightmare look off your face."

With that, they threw back their heads and held their bellies as they roared with laughter.

As Heather rested in her bed, she thought, *What is this new anticipation I feel? A change is coming, but I don't know what it could be. Could it be that just one vacation has given me a positive flow of energy I've never felt before? Especially since I've been in this wheelchair, I have secretly felt a little downhearted, never really wanting to share that emotion. Is time really on my side? Is time sending me something new?*

She closed her eyes but not to sleep. She felt this would be a good time to send out a prayer. As she pulled her blanket around her, she felt a breeze fill the room. She knew in her heart that her prayer had been received, and her eyes grew heavier and her mind swirled with the beautiful chaos of a new dream.

By the time the week ended, and Heather returned home, she felt renewed. She thought as she returned to her desk, *All the memories that came to mind during vacation, the accident and then the wheelchair, I have to continue my work to help others with spinal damage.*

She channeled her memories into a wonderfully obsessive way of working on experiments to help others, and she began working more with stem cells with the DNA. This was the dedication and desire of her heart. She was ready with refreshed hopes for her life and a new focus on her job.

Now that vacation was over, she was happy to return to her apartment. As she got herself ready for sleep, she went into her closet and found her jewelry box. She knew what she wanted to see; it had been a while since she had last held her shell. She brought it to her mirror and put the gold chain and shell around her neck. It glimmered with the same shine she remembered from when she had first seen it. As she stared at its reflection, a flame in her soul revived.

Chapter 10
Decisions

Four years had passed for Cove as he had been studying under the watchful eye of Dr. B. at the Moscow Hospital of Special Surgery. He was proud of the training he had received in the hospital of special surgery and especially grateful his friend John had followed through in his acceptance to the hospital, where they both began their internship just three months after graduation. One morning, Cove was making his rounds and checking up on Dr. B's last surgery patient, Mr. Nanda.

"Good morning, Mr. Nanda," he said as he approached the man's bed. "I see that all your vitals are normal. You're doing well after the insertion of the interspinous process spacer. Since you only needed one spacer, the surgery wasn't as long as we anticipated." Cove read his chart and took out a penlight to check his eyes, then checked his blood pressure. Although a bit dazed from the anesthesia, Mr. Nanda was still able to respond to Cove, "I feel just a little nauseous, but other than that, I do feel a difference in my back. I have a little less pain."

Cove looked up from his writing in the chart and wondered what accent he was hearing.

"Mr. Nanda, you have a very nice accent. From what country did you travel?"

Mr. Nanda gave a sigh and raised his eyes toward Cove. "I have traveled from a poor town outside of Mumbai, India, called Wadala. Mumbai began its commercial center on the basis of textile mills. I worked as a tailor there all my life. Then, when some of our relatives traveled here to Russia, we decided to follow."

He then shifted a little to get more comfortable. Cove moved closer in anticipation to hear more of his life story.

"We arrived here thirty years ago with my wife and two children. I have continued with my skill here in Russia as a tailor. Always busy, so much to do, and very happy that I can do so. But last week while lifting heavy boxes filled with material, a sharp pain shot down my back, and I fell to the floor. That's when the ambulance took me here."

Cove enjoyed listening to Mr. Nanda about his travel to Moscow, so he decided to be more inquisitive. "I'm thinking you traveled here in about 1950? Very brave of you to make that decision with two babies." He steadily held on to Mr. Nanda's chart while intensely listening to his story.

"Well, it was at that time that Nikita Khrushchev changed his doctrine of peaceful coexistence, which brought Soviet-American relations to a new high and also added India air flights to Russia."

"Great history lesson, Mr. Nanda. Since you have been here in Russia for decades, could you explain what it was like to live in Mumbai?"

"Oh, I would love to explain a little about my old country. Mumbai was once called Bombay. In 1995, the name was officially changed when Shiv Sena came into power. Since Bombay was thought of as a legacy of British colonialism, he wanted the name to reflect its Maratha heritage, hence it was renamed Mumbai."

Cove became more intrigued with his patient's explanation of the name change but wanted other information.

"How does Mumbai compare to New York City?"

"Well, I think since Mumbai is an important region of India, New York would hold the same elements. Mumbai is called the City of Dreams. New York is called the Big Apple. They are closely related, filled with merchants and people in search of work and a better career."

Mr. Nanda's life story and the history of his country became fascinating to Cove. He became intrigued with the thought of the City of Dreams and comparing it to the Big Apple. Cove was eager to get home after he finished his rounds for the day. Back at the apartment, he found a world map that was hidden between his books he always reread for surgical information. He opened it up and found Mr. Nanda's country, India. Knowing Wadala is a poor part of Mumbai, he started wondering if there was much need for surgical teams there. Within a few days of researching about doctors traveling to India, he found a low rate of surgical doctors in the country, especially in this one particular hospital just outside of Mumbai in the town of Wadala. He wondered if he should pursue this unexpected reaction to Mumbai. A sudden warmth came over him, and he knew this urge to follow his inclination was real. It became his desire, and in that desire, his thoughts went back to an image of Heather.

I've traveled over the globe to Russia, now India. She could never find me, or has she ever given me a thought? Oh, what a ridiculous thought. This is just a useless memory. Why oh why am I thinking of her again?

***

John was the perfect friend, someone who Cove trusted to talk this over with. It was like old times in high school when they questioned and answered each other when there was a problem with a girl or schoolwork. They were good memories. He invited John to meet at the local café.

"My thoughts are like driving around the same block over and over and faster and faster. I just had to talk it over with you, buddy." He looked at John as if he were about to ask a question.

"Hey, Cove, anytime. What's bothering you? Looks serious." John took a sip of his cappuccino and sat back to listen.

"Since my conversation with Mr. Nanda, and after I researched his town of Wadala, I truly feel led to go there and help. I haven't told anyone yet, and I have a meeting with Dr. B. for advice. I just wanted you to know that I believe I am on my way to another country." Cove tapped his cup of coffee and waited for his friend's honest response.

"Listen, our journey started when we graduated high school and came here to Russia together. We've worked side by side and helped our patients heal remarkably. I'm excited and happy for your decision. I would ask to go with you, but I truly feel this is the place where I am supposed to

121

be. This is your future. For some reason, it's where you should be. I give you my blessings. Just keep in touch with me. Give me updates and pictures!" John got up and gave him a bear hug.

They spent the rest of the evening sharing all they had learned while studying under Dr. B. and becoming doctors.

"Hey, remember our first meeting with Dr. B? He was talking like a military soldier. I looked over at you, and your face was stone white." John laughed and gave Cove a little punch in the shoulder.

"Oh yeah, what a moment that was. I remember it clearly, but you know, I believe it is his strength in surgery and teaching that made us become the top surgeons. I'll be forever thankful that I have been accepted to this teaching hospital."

They clinked their coffee cups together and were thankful. That night when Cove went home, he found his mind wandering to this small town called Wadala and the information Mr. Nanda had given him during their conversation. The pictures of people living there that he had found in his research could not leave his thoughts—images of patients with disfigured backs because they could not afford surgery.

***

It was early—8 a.m.—just before Dr. B's first surgery of the day. Dr. B. sat tapping his pen on the desk, finding the words to say about traveling to India. He gave Cove an understanding look as he rubbed his chin in thought.

"Your questions take me back to the time I first started my internship at a small hospital overseas. I wanted to start my profession abroad while experiencing a new culture firsthand. There comes a time when pushing one's ideas that could save our world becomes morally the right thing to do. You will find the opportunity of immersing yourself in a foreign culture to be an invaluable experience. Here in Russia, you learned our culture and new advanced techniques. You will be able to bring all this new knowledge pertaining to the spinal cord to those in need in Wadala. I wholeheartedly support and agree with your decision." He extended his arm for a professional handshake to confirm his agreement.

"Thank you, Dr. B. After speaking to your patient Mr. Nanda, I feel led to go abroad to Wadala and practice and teach the techniques I have learned here in Moscow while under the direction of your expertise. I found the rural areas like Wadala have a high need of surgery at the small facility located there. I believe I am needed there."

"Absolutely! It was a great experience for me, and it will be for you. This will be a refreshing part of working in a new system and helping others on the road to recovery. I will help in the documentation needed for you to begin the process. I still have colleagues in different countries, as well as the small town of Wadala in Mumbai. Let me make a phone call and get you on the road." Dr. B. laughed, realizing he had made a play on words. "I mean on a jet!"

***

About six weeks later all the arrangements were made, from the flight, to having one of the staff meet him at the airport and take him to his new destination, Wadala. Cove had just finished assisting Dr. B. in surgery when he heard his name being announced over the PA system. "Dr. Ferris, you are wanted in the conference room. Dr. Ferris, you are wanted in the conference room."

Cove was confused because he didn't know he was supposed to attend a meeting, so he texted John to ask him if he knew of one, but there was no response. He moved along the hallway to the conference room, but the door wouldn't open. He gave it one hard shove, opening it to vivid colors of balloons and all his colleagues yelling, "Congratulations!"

His mouth hung open, and he shook his head as the shock registered on his face.

John ran over to him and gave him a bear hug, then placed a cardboard crown on his head.

"Well, my old friend, we crown you king of the week before you leave us. I took some of your surgeries to free up the last couple of days of your stay with us. Come on now, each one of us brought our own special homemade dish to celebrate. Okay, everyone, make way for our king."

John walked his friend to the table while the crowd gave a round of applause.

"Hey, John, I can't believe you all did this for me. You know surprise isn't an emotion I've ever dealt with well. But this is outstanding. I feel like I could jump to the moon."

They laughed with joy and tears. There were sounds of clicking glasses as John made a toast.

"Dr. Ferris and I have never had to say goodbye. We went through junior high and high school together and graduated together. We had the honor of being accepted to this most prestigious teaching hospital here in Moscow. We learned under the guidance and supervision of Dr. B. But it's time not to say goodbye to my brother, but to remember and treasure the grandest memories of working together. So, we are not forced to say goodbye, but to wish you more success in the healing art of surgery. I leave you with my favorite quote from Hippocrates: 'Wherever the art of medicine is loved, there is also a love of humanity.' And Dr. Ferris, this is what you hold in your heart."

John found his throat was choking up, and he could not speak any longer. He turned away and took a drink to calm himself.

Then Dr. B. held up his glass and made a few jokes to lighten the mood.

"If ever a scalpel could talk, it would remind us of a new surgical hand with its first shaky cut. No, that's not true. Dr. Ferris has been our finest surgeon, and although he will be greatly missed, we send him off with our blessings. He will help those in great need in Wadala. He will treat and heal many with his expertise. We will miss you."

Chapter 11
Mission

Two months later, Cove finally had the opportunity to work shoulder to shoulder with Dr. Frances, an old friend and colleague of Dr. B's. Dr. Frances was both a proficient neurosurgeon and orthopedic surgeon, and he had become renowned in his profession. Being a seasoned doctor, he was also considered a teaching doctor to the staff. It wasn't too often that he would receive a request from interns to study at the hospital in Wadala. He knew of the need for more surgeons and was exhilarated when he had received the call from Dr. B. that one of his surgeons from Russia was on his way to assist him, for Dr. Frances was the only one who was able to perform spinal cord surgery at the hospital. He often wondered when another doctor would come to help him in this part of the world.

When Cove arrived, he said, "Dr. Ferris, I am so grateful that you made the decision to come to this little town of Wadala to help with this much-needed spinal surgery. This is the calling card to heighten your profession. Whatever is ahead will be a great challenge, but you will see great results."

It was like a pandemic. Dr. Frances and Dr. Ferris plus the field united turned the outside area into pop-up hospitals to help with the overflow of patients in dire need. The main hospital was little more than a very large house, filled with medical staff and supplies. The nurses hurried purposefully from room to room, patient to patient. Cove could hear moans from an adjacent bed and knew that would be his next patient.

There was a woman with a broken pelvis lying in the next bed. He walked over to her with care and compassion. The medical staff never wavered in their genuine concern in spite of the lack of help. One time, there was a car accident where a woman had to be rushed into the hospital. She was driving and had lost control of the wheel, spinning into a street divider. After Cove examined her, he found the force of the accident had caused a disc to shift. He wanted her to be his next patient when there was the sudden sound of the old ambulance coming into the ER station. Cove ran to meet it and find out what had happened.

The EMT met with Cove. "This man is unconscious. He was working on the roof of a building and fell to the ground."

Cove quickly made an examination. "There is swelling and bruising in the lower part of his spine. Let's get him to X-ray and find out more, then we can see if he needs surgery."

Accidents and emergencies were everywhere. And there were those with bent backs, spinal disfigurements, and scoliosis deformities who needed expert surgery. It was all there in front of him. As his eyes filled with compassion for the suffering, he knew the purpose of being in Wadala, the source of his desire to serve.

This is my mission—one of them, at least—in order to achieve something for others. It warms my inner core to help and cure others and fan this internal flame, Cove thought as he did the surgeries with Dr. Frances, who shared his knowledge with Cove. The two were able to help an abundance of patients to be able to walk and return to their employment. Unceasingly, they worked. Time never entered their mind. Day in, day out, they relentlessly worked for the good of the cure.

There was an emergency one morning. Both doctors were attending to so many patients when two parents came rushing in with their daughter. She was carried into the entrance of the small hospital, lying across both their arms.

One of the attendees helped them in and put the young girl on a gurney, then called for Dr. Frances. After his examination, he sent her for an MRI. After the results came in, he went to find Cove.

"Dr. Ferris, she has what is called an intradural tumor. It is a spinal tumor that begins within the spinal cord or covering the spinal cord. It's affecting the bones of the spine. This young girl is only sixteen. Her name is Sheena. Her family works as farmers outside of town. She has been working with them and she has been feeling pain in her back for months, so they thought she had sprained her back. When she couldn't get out of bed, they carried her here. They cannot afford the surgery, and they need our help. Here are the MRI reports. It's a good thing we bought that machine last year." Dr. Frances handed over the documents.

Once Cove had carefully read through the report, he agreed they needed to perform immediate surgery. Sheena's parents were sitting in the small waiting room of the hospital. It was an old room; the carpet had a dingy color of faded gray with small ripples in it that needed to be pulled back and fixed. Holding on to each other's hands, they rocked back and forth in prayer.

"Excuse me, are you Sheena's parents?" Cove waited, hoping they understood his language.

They spoke in a broken English but enough where they could communicate with the doctors. "Yes, yes, Doctor, please tell us what happened to our Sheena. She could not move. We didn't know what to do." Sheena's father spoke with a steady breath, trying to stay calm, but he couldn't control his hands.

"I have the report, and it shows a tumor was growing in her spine, which caused her mobility to stop. We are preparing her right now for surgery. It will be a while. I suggest you go home and wait where you will be more comfortable than sitting in these steel chairs. One of us will come to your home and take you back here to see your daughter. Is that okay with you?"

They agreed because the waiting room was old and uncomfortable, especially since they were so tired from beginning their work at sunrise and ending at dusk.

"Sheena is our eldest. She is so full of life, loves to explore, is always reading books she finds at the village library. And we have another daughter and son waiting at home. We appreciate if you would come to us when the surgery is done." Sheena's mother continued to hold on to her husband's shaky hands then closed her eyes, hiding her tears.

They walked out holding on to each other and helping each other stand since they both felt weak knowing their daughter had to undergo this type of surgery.

Surgery was set for that afternoon. The scrub team's voices spread out requesting instruments and giving instructions. The anesthetist sat above the patient while the runner nurse kept the operating room safe with antibacterial disinfectant. Even though Dr. Frances' voice was slightly muffled by his mask, he was still able to convey to Cove what this surgery would entail.

The operating room suddenly became quiet. The two surgeons stood opposite each other, looking over Sheena's back. They were ready. Then Dr. Frances spoke.

"I have a quote for you before we begin: 'He who wishes to be a surgeon should go to war.' Hippocrates. This is one of the quotes I learned while studying for my medical exams a long time ago."

"I agree, Dr. Frances. We have been fighting a war on diseases, patients lying on beds in corridors, surgeries on little children, and now a tumor in a young girl. Yes, this is a battle, but we are warriors, combating anything that enters this hospital."

Cove made the first incision over the section of the spine and down to the arch of the vertebra.

Dr. Frances continued to hold open the section with a clamp.

"There it is. I am going to remove it in one piece," Cove said. His hands were steady as the nurse carefully wiped his forehead. The room was cold, but the doctors could feel the internal heat from their nerves.

Dr. Frances glanced up at the clock. They had already been in surgery for five hours. He hoped this young girl could withstand all this time.

"It is wrapped around one vertebra, but I will cut one side of it and remove it, then go to the other side and remove the remainder. Then I will perform a fusion to set the vertebrae together." Cove was composed and confident, never taking his eyes off the procedure.

Dr. Frances continued to suction and help guide the instrument used to remove the tumor.

Eight hours had now passed, and the surgery was a success. Sheena was in recovery, and the nurse stayed by her side until she woke up. Then Cove walked in.

"Hello, Sheena. You will be able to sit up tomorrow morning. This nurse will not leave you. She will help you to walk a little tomorrow. Your skin color looks healthy, and your eyes are clear. You did well, young lady."

She was still in a daze from the anesthesia and pain medication but was able to slowly speak. "Thank you, Dr. Ferris. Thank you for all that you do here. I would have never thought that I would have a tumor. It was frightening at first, but now I am glad that you fixed it. I really want to see my parents." She looked up at him with an unsmiling face.

"Not to worry. Someone just left to go get them. They can stay a couple of hours, then we will take them home. You need to rest so your body heals. All is well."

Cove held her hand for a moment, then left. He was pleased with the outcome of the surgery for her. He was happy that he could continue to help those in great need.

One particular morning, there was a phone call for Dr. Frances. He rushed over to the front desk and was on the phone for about a half hour. Then he hung up and ran to find Cove.

"Dr. Ferris, you won't believe this! Your prayers have come true. I just received a phone call from the World Bank. Their mission is to help end poverty and promote shared prosperity, and they have decided to give us a grant! We will be able to treat more of the underprivileged patients, construct new hospital wards, build rest houses, and provide medicines." Dr. Frances usually never displayed his feelings, but this triggered an abundance of emotions for him. There was a flame in his heart that melted his outer exterior.

Cove's heart beat faster, and there was a buzzing in his brain at the excitement of what he had just heard. "Dr. Frances, I see what is happening here. We can add on an entire extension to the hospital, a whole new wing." He had to stop for a moment. He leaned against the reception desk and drew in a lungful of air. His eyes glimmered. He was overwhelmed with joy.

Within the next six months, they were able to take down the outside pop-up tents. Requests from new interns from other countries came flooding in wanting to intern at the new, expanded hospital where they set training classes into action. The facility was able to house the interns as well as nurses. In over one year, the facility also advanced in its surgical team.

Cove was glad he had listened to the inner passion he felt. The desire of his heart was fulfilled. He was now able to help more of the people of Wadala. In his heart, it was all for Mr. Nanda.

***

Three years had passed, and Cove was completely consumed with his dream of working in Wadala. He thought about a relationship he had had with one of the nurses that had turned sour. At first, he was thrilled with her feisty confidence, which had later turned to aggressiveness. His thoughts turned to Heather.

I don't know why I'm comparing her with Heather. Even at ten, Heather was feisty but gentle. I haven't met anyone with eyes like hers. It was so many years ago. I wonder what her personality is like now and where she is. I don't even know her last name. Her memory haunts me.

This one particular morning, just before he was ready to leave for the hospital, Cove received a phone call from his mother. There was an emergency with his dad. He had suffered a heart attack but was safely in the ICU unit being monitored by a heart specialist. Cove knew it was time to get back home to be with his parents because he had been away since his internship in Moscow with just a few holiday breaks home in between. In that moment, he made the decision to fly home and take a sabbatical.

There was a roller coaster of emotions that washed over the doctors and staff who had grown to love and respect

Cove. Everyone admired how he had helped working with the engineering services department in designing his dream with the construction of the new hospital wing. Dr. Frances held the blue ribbon at the unveiling of the addition for the ribbon-cutting event. All were present: colleagues, staff, the construction supervisors, and even some patients.

Within a couple of months, they all said their goodbyes and sent him home with their blessings. Dr. Frances moved to Cove and grabbed his hand, and in an emotional moment, he said his goodbye.

"Dr. Ferris, what great achievements for others you have created here. Because you felt it was right, you made it right for others. Your passion that went from a spark to a bonfire within you has helped this hospital not only to restore patients but our building. Thank you for your energy and humanity. Job well done, young man. Now go home and take care of your family. You will be entirely missed here." He became speechless and turned away to hide the emotions rising up.

The staff made sure to have a going-away party for Cove. The private staff lunchroom was set up with balloons and sandwiches. Doctors and nurses made their way to give final hugs and blessings to Cove. Cove was especially surprised to see some of his patients walk in to say farewell. As he watched Sheena and the man who had fallen off the roof and many others walking toward him, he felt the enemy of spinal injuries had been defeated, the battle was over, and the surgeries had been a success.

***

A sixteen-hour flight gave Cove much time to think. A maze of thoughts filled his mind. He was worried about his father's health and not being near his parents while they reached their elderly years. He thought about his own life, how he had reached the age of maturity, and he had accomplished much. He was proud that he was a part of the restoration of the human body. He loved his profession, but the years had passed so quickly, and as he had grown older, he had found himself missing the comfort of his home at Glen Cove. At this point in his career, he had already traveled the world and was not now committed to any hospital. He thought to himself, *My dreams have been fulfilled, but where is my next path? What is in store for my future?*

Finally, he landed at John F. Kennedy airport. Mary was waiting at the arrival gate when she saw him dragging his luggage toward her. She jumped out and ran to him.

"Oh, Cove, thank God you're home. We need you now. Dad asks for you every day." Her silent weeping shook her voice as she held on to her son.

"I know, Mom. I'm home now. Let's just get to the hospital. I can always unpack later."

Glen Cove Hospital had an odor of bleach as they ran through the corridor, bringing to his mind the memories of the hospital in Wadala. He thought of his colleagues and the atmosphere of healing his patients. The reception desk was loud with phones ringing and visitors running back and forth for information about their families, yet the nurses moved unhurried and purposefully from room to room. There was a clatter of questions from families asking about relatives or friends who had been admitted. It was a bubble of noise that engulfed him, capturing his brain and making it impossible to gather his thoughts about his father. He thought, *I have to find the cardiologist before I get to Dad's room. I need more information. I have to know what's really going on with him.*

As he walked down the hallway, he saw a doctor standing just in front of his dad's room. He said, "Excuse me. My name is Dr. Ferris. I'm his son. I flew in when I got the call about his heart."

Dr. Warchol stopped reading the chart and turned to Cove. He acknowledged Cove with a shake of their hands.

"Oh yes, Dr. Ferris, your mom spoke with me when your dad was admitted. It is a pleasure to meet you, even under these circumstances."

Cove stood with a blank look on his face and squeezed his arms around himself, trying to hold himself together. "Please tell me, what is your diagnosis? Will he be alright?"

"I just received all the results and was just going over them. The echocardiogram results are here. His LDL cholesterol and triglycerides are much too high. There is also an eighty percent blockage in the LAD artery, short for left anterior descending artery, which led to a mild heart attack. Also, the echocardiogram results show his heart muscle is a little weak. We must do a bypass surgery and insert a stent. This will hold it open and push away any plaque. Then he will be fine and can resume his activities. I will start him on a common blood thinner called Warfarin and also Vasotec to treat his high blood pressure. After a week here, we will see the results, and then I want him in my office every week to monitor him until I think I can reduce any medications. He must have activity, like a long walk every day."

Cove nervously paid close attention to each word coming from the doctor but believed his dad would do fine. Mary stood there taking in all the information as well, but she felt like her mind was skipping some of the words. She started feeling weak, and her face became flushed. Then Cove realized she was starting to sway and took her to a nearby seat and gave her water.

Cove spoke gently to her and held her hand. "Mom, are you okay? Please don't get sick now. We need to get into his room and see him. He's waiting for us."

"I know, son. I'm better now. It was just a sudden shock to hear so much. I know I have to be strong to take care of him. Oh, Cove, you came home just in time to help me with all this. I feel so overwhelmed."

"No worries, Mom. Come on, let's get in there."

As he entered his dad's room, he noticed a few vases of flowers on his table from the many friends he had made over the years. Then he saw his dad lying in his bed, and a sudden feeling of gloom entered his body. He could feel dampness seeping into his pores. Then like a child, he reached out and touched his dad's fingers. He thought, *Holding his hand, I feel the comfort and the kindness that's always there for me. We belong together. Oh Lord, please keep our family together. Bring him back to life.*

For a couple of hours, Cove and Mary sat right beside his dad, afraid to leave him for a minute. But as Cove continued to hold his hand and pray, his dad suddenly moved. Then his eyes slowly opened, and through a haze, he saw Cove.

"Dr. Ferris," his dad softly called out with a half-smile as Cove tightly held on to his hand. Cove felt the muscles of his neck tense as he gripped it.

"Dad, I just talked to your cardiologist. He gave me permission to read through your tests and explain to you what should be done. He is going to do a simple procedure. One of your arteries is eighty percent blocked. This is why you experienced a heart attack. The surgeon will have to do a bypass and stenting, which will allow the blood to flow better. You should be fine after that. Please don't worry and stay calm. This is an easy procedure, and Mom and I will be waiting right outside in the waiting room. You will see us immediately after the surgery."

Cove searched his dad's eyes for a gleam of understanding. His father nodded yes even though he felt the adrenaline flow through his system and fearful thoughts of surgery swirled in his mind.

The next morning, Cove and Mary sat in the waiting room. It was a typical hospital room, sparse and functional, with the usual TV set that hung from the wall. The constant sound of the everyday news blaring with boring commercials mixed into his thoughts. The gray of the walls fused into the gray carpet, leaving Cove to envision a gray cloud hovering over him. Cove felt a little anxious about his dad. They sat watching but not hearing a sound as hours passed.

After five hours, there was the rustling sound of doctor's scrubs. Cove and Mary quickly looked up.

Dr. Warchol walked over to where they were sitting, still covered from head to toe in his scrubs with a smile on his face. "Excuse me, Dr. Ferris. The surgery is over."

138

Cove jumped up and reached out to shake hands with the doctor. He asked with nervous anticipation, "Please, tell me how it all went."

"Your father is in excellent condition, which made the surgery move quickly and precisely. He is in recovery now, but in less than an hour, you will both be able to visit him. I'll send the nurse at that time to bring you in. You will notice as the days go by that he will have more vitality. I had to bring you the good news right away. For now, just sit and try to make yourself comfortable. Trust me, he will be fine; my staff and I will take good care of him."

Cove's dad was still under the sedative as they entered his room, but he must have felt their presence. He lazily rolled open his glazed eyes as he heard the squeak of sneakers and spoke with a pleasing, gravelly voice. "Hey, son, looks like I made it through. Hon, I can barely see you. Come closer."

"Dear, you look so tired. You need plenty of rest. We won't stay. I just wanted to see you and make sure you were alright. The nurses here will take great care of you. We will come back tomorrow. Right now, I would feel better myself knowing that you are sleeping this off." Mary kissed his forehead and held him for a moment. Then they left.

Each day during that week in the hospital, Cove saw his father strengthen on the road to wellness. He noticed a sense of relief his father showed because the symptoms of chest pain and shortness of breath were resolved. Then, for a few weeks, his father remained in the cardiac rehab program, where he received regular exercise. This helped in building muscle and stamina, which showed in the way he now walked. His cardiologist made daily visits to ensure all was going well. Cove watched as his mom walked him up and down the hospital hallway. He thought, *They have a strong bond of love. She loves taking care of him. I hope to have that same love someday.*

His dad said, "Son, thank you for bringing Mom here every day. I made a vow to myself that when I leave here, I will set up a small gym in our basement. I have so many ideas. A Nordic walking treadmill and a stationary bike. And I'll definitely get your mom on one of those machines. We will get healthy together!" He held on to his wife and gave her a special, tender look.

"Well, that sounds great! You'll be coming home in a few more days. I am so grateful that this is over, and you will be fine again. I was scared at first, Dad, but I remember all that you have given to me. If I were to make receipts for every good thing you had ever done for me, I wouldn't have enough prescription pads!"

With that said, their laughter overflowed into the air and down the hallway. Then they huddled and cried joyfully.

The next day, the surgeon walked in to check on his patient and signed the release form for his dad to go home. After checking off his chart, he turned to Cove.

"Dr. Ferris, I did some research on your medical history. You certainly have become successful with spinal cord surgery. It's amazing how you traveled to Moscow straight from high school. And I see that after years of training under the guidance from Dr. Brezukaev, you then traveled to Wadala, Mumbai. You helped so many patients in Wadala. And you worked so hard together with Dr. Frances to get the new specialized surgical wing completed." He spoke with a spark of wonder in his tone.

"Oh yes, it took much diligence to get it finalized, but it was well worth it. Dr. Frances was agreeable from the time we took on our first patient. I am so grateful to him for all that he does and that he was so easy to work with," Cove said with a steady smile of deep satisfaction.

"You know, we could use your expertise here in Long Island. This is a not only a cardiovascular hospital but we also are affiliated with The Spine Hospital at Mount Sinai. Our hospitals need to achieve a quota of junior doctors to maintain the teaching status in conjunction with the spine institute. Plus, we have a great many patients in need of spinal surgery. There are so many cases from congenital spine abnormalities, car accidents, disease, and countless other causes. Seriously, would you consider becoming a part of our team?"

It took a second or two for this question to register in Cove's mind. Finally, the information sank in. Cove's eyes became larger, and with arched eyebrows, he quickly answered. "Doctor, I am amazed at this invitation. During the plane ride coming back home to New York, I was feeling I should return, but I didn't really know where this feeling was coming from or where I would even begin to investigate to start. Well, you just answered what was on my mind."

It was obvious that this surgeon had a proud kind of grace that shone from his face. Cove thought of him as a person whose ideas would save the world. Cove thought, *He could be considered a healer. He provides his patients with health for the body and soul and care with a medicinal level of love, even with how he has continued to check in with my dad. I can see it in his eyes. There's a softer spark than when*

I first met him. The professional man was gone for a moment. Instead, I saw the eyes of one who loves his patients.

Then Mary threw her arms around her son's neck, squeezing him tightly as tears dropped onto his shoulder.

"Oh, my son, these are two miracles. Dad is healed, and now you will be with us as we grow old!"

The following week, Cove met with the Dr. McGuiness, chief neurosurgeon at The Spine Hospital at Mount Sinai. His office was as meticulous as his reputation. He counted all the framed degrees that were neatly placed around the room on the white walls. He thought to himself as he sat and inspected the room, *Everything is just so. The walls, the chairs, even his desk. It's a nice alabaster-type of resin, but a very modern curved structure for a very seasoned doctor.*

At that moment, the doctor entered the room. He was aging, and his dream of retirement was coming closer, but he was deeply concerned for his hospital. He felt the need to form a small team of teachers.

"Dr. Ferris, what a pleasure to meet you. Your résumé speaks loudly. We rarely find a candidate who has so much experience as you have. You learned from the best, Dr. Frances and Dr. Brezukaev, who have the greatest reputations. You are highly qualified. I have been wanting to start a team of interns and top surgeons to work with in cytogenesis. I'll give you some information about Dr. Storm and her work with DNA. She has published many articles, and the great news is the *New York Times* published an article about her work. I would like you to select a group that is the best in terms of attentiveness, knowledge, maturity, and skill and develop a team to go work with Dr.

Storm and her associates—interns, junior doctors, doctors you know and can trust. Teach them to focus on the needs of each patient. Review what you find at The New York Microbiology Laboratory with Dr. Harris, who is the chief clinical microbiology lab director. Introduce these young doctors to this type of pathology and practice."

"Doctor, I can efficiently put together a notable team for you. I also have a friend in mind who has been in Moscow under the leadership of Dr. Brezukaev. I would like to offer him a place on our team, if you don't mind."

"Of course, Dr. Ferris. If he studied with you and Dr. B., I am positive he will add greatness to our team and that his reputation must be without flaw."

When the discussion was over, the two men shook hands and thanked each other. Cove rushed home. He had to make the call to his dear friend John Frank.

***

"Hey, John, how's it going out there in my old hometown of Moscow?" Cove gave a laugh at the thought of Moscow being one of his homes and added the thought of Mumbai as another.

John sat in his office chair, swiveling around. "Oh, Cove, it's great to finally hear your voice. It's been way too long. Going good here. There have been a lot of surgeries, but all have been successful. I think I'm getting overtired, though, but well, what can I say? I'm here and doing a successful job with my patients, working from my heart to help."

"Well, old friend, I have an offer for you. I have been offered a place here in New York with The Spine Hospital at Mount Sinai in Manhattan. I met the cardiologist who is taking care of my father, and he mentioned the need. I aced the interview, and I am now the head director of surgery. The main key here is that I have to gather a team of interns with an equal number of surgeons to accompany the team at the diagnostic lab. I mentioned your name, and the chief surgeon said to please call you and they'll fly you in." Cove held his breath in anticipation.

"I can't believe it. An offer to work with you? Just like the old times here in Russia. You know I've been thinking about being back in New York for a while now. It's been so long that I've been away. Every time I call home or take a vacation break there, my mom cries. That makes me more homesick. I have been thinking, 'What could I do or where could I apply in New York?' God worked through you, Cove. I'm giving you a deafening yes!" John was spinning in his revolving chair with one arm in the air.

"Alright! We'll be working together again like in the beginning. Seems like life has a way of reconnecting people. I'll make all the arrangements and get back to you with the details. You will need to have a serious talk with Dr. B. I know it will be hard for him to let you go."

Cove quickly hung up the phone and got to work on the arrangements for getting his best friend back home. He was thrilled that they would be working together again after so many years having gone by. A month later, all was arranged.

John was asked to join a few residents in the main auditorium. To his surprise, there were more than just a few.

It seemed the entire hospital was there with well wishes for him. There were a thousand goodbyes, tears, and hugs. The staff took turns between shifts to offer congratulations and to reminiscence about the special friendships they had made with him. John felt that the room never emptied, but just kept refilling like an empty glass of wine. Finally, at the end of the day Dr. B. took a place at the podium to speak.

"There will be a great loss here in Moscow. Even so, I send you home, dear Dr. Frank, with my blessing and the warmth of the sun to impart to those in your new environment helping and healing all those in need. Your expertise will definitely help with the new team of doctors. But remember, this will always be your home away from home." Dr. B. stepped down, his tongue gnawing at the roof of his parched mouth, hungering for liquid. His eyes shifted a little to the side, checking if anyone noticed the glassy layer in his eyes.

"Thank you, Dr. B., and everyone here at this farewell party. I take these emotions with me, these memories where I grew with comfort and joy. I am at a loss for words, my dear friends, my family. We will keep in touch. And yes, this will always be my home away from home."

Later that evening, as he began to pack his suitcase, he held the airline tickets and his passport in his hands. Looking down at all the information he needed to leave, he thought, *Today, I feel happy to know that I will be back with my family and my good friend. I don't think anyone can tell the combination of anxiety and sadness I feel. But I know this choice was handed to me at the right moment.*

John remained deep in thought with all the mixed feelings he had about leaving one family behind but returning to his own family and friends. He knew everything was moving in the right direction at the right time. His thoughts turned to the first time he had met Dr. B. He had posed as a soldier and appeared brusque, but John had soon learned that under the façade was a doctor wanting to educate and instruct his new interns. He remembered when Dr. B. had handed him about seven pages of instructions for learning diagnosis, surgery, and labs. He was responsible for patients he had never met before. John was upset and felt it was way too much for a new intern. But after a month, he realized the importance of knowing all there was to begin his internship. Then he knew Dr. B. was looking for the best in his interns.

There was another thought of a funny time with all the new interns he had just made friends with.

I remember my first time in the operating room with Dr. B. He was standing next to the patient, gown and all. All my new friends were there, ready to learn the procedure for this patient. I began speaking loudly, reviewing my surgical checklist with the nurses.

"Okay, we have the surgical equipment, the machines are clean, everyone is in place. Patient is safely under anesthesia. I think this is a go-ahead."

Dr. B. said, "You wait until now to figure this stuff out?" and then he just laughed. He really helped me to lighten the moment. I'll always appreciate him and miss him.

He remembered all the surgeries Dr. B. had taught him, one especially. A small child was born with congenital scoliosis. Dr. B. was telling the staff that this child's vertebrae had not formed normally before the baby's birth. The baby was sent by ambulance to Moscow Hospital of Special Surgery. Dr. B. had firmly said, "We must do surgery immediately. We do not want this child to by definition become disabled. Dr. Frank, you will assist me. Let's scrub."

John thought, *This child is a wonderful gift in my hands, I must help and heal.* He held his hands steady with each incision and went deep into the vertebrae. He knew exactly what to do and with much precision was able to completely correct the issue. When it was over, everyone in the operating room cheered. Later that day, some doctors talked to John, telling him he had saved a baby's life and he would be a great surgeon.

Time felt endless for John as he sat in his seat on his air flight to New York. He thought, *This is such a strange occurrence. Here I am, heading home. I've missed my parents so much. Now we will all be together again: my family, Cove's family, and all our church members.*

The sky turned royal blue, then it faded into darkness, lulling John into a comfortable sleep. For the next sixteen hours the jetliner soared through the sky, he had time to dream.

Chapter 12
The Interview

Heather's morning was moving slowly as she sipped her coffee and got ready to leave for work. She then received a phone call from the *New York Times*. All her articles she had published in the *Scientific Journals* had been reviewed by this one journalist named Russell. She had read some of his work, and there was a side picture of the journalist. With his dark hair and black eyeglasses, she thought of him as the fictional character Clark Kent in the movie *Superman*. She admired his way of gaining wider perspectives for his readers and his way of explaining complex information at a simple, digestible level as if he were a therapist. He was the number one journalist at the *New York Times*, and he was calling her!

"Good morning, Heather! My name is Russell, and I'm from the *New York Times*. I'm very interested in a few of your published articles I've read, and I'd like to make an appointment to interview you for my report on your perspectives. I'd appreciate if I could meet you in person and review all of your published discoveries. Would you mind setting a date and time?"

She nervously invited him to join her that evening at her home. Later that night, they sat comfortably in her living room. She knew there would be many questions during this interview, so she had put out coffee and cookies to help keep the mood relaxed.

"Heather, the pen of a journalist is meant to show the invisible walls of your research to the public. I want to unveil and give a wider perspective on the meaning of your studies for doctors who are interested in the healing of their patients."

Russell knew exactly how to explain to her what he wanted to publish. He had graduated at the top of his class with his master's in investigative journalism. He was offered many positions from different newspapers around the country, but his first choice had been the *New York Times*, and he had accepted immediately. Working at the *Times*, he had learned how to hunt down documents and write his story. He had become its leading journalist, publishing front-page articles, the most important stories in the news.

"Thank you for allowing me to spend this quality time with you. First, tell me a little about your life growing up. When did this desire to study science begin?" he asked with his pad and pen ready, studying her every gesture.

"Well, as a little girl, my parents always took me to our family beach in New Jersey. I found myself so intrigued with the seagulls, how they flew overhead just for some crumbs of bread. I always wondered how their wings would spread so wide. Then I became inquisitive about the seashells I found. I always questioned, could a living thing live inside a shell? What made these animals so alive?" She leaned back momentarily and giggled, moving her slender, manicured hands with each word.

"Very interesting for a little girl to be so curious. Can I ask you a personal question?"

Heather already knew where this was going and was very prepared to answer, even though it would involve recalling a suppressed memory.

"Sure, I'm an open book." She sat with her arms crossed and hands clasped tightly, subconsciously creating a barrier between them.

"Heather, at what time in your life did you have to face your physical challenge?" His eyes steadily held hers, eager to learn something.

"Well, it certainly was a challenge. I was only ten at the time. It was a hit-and-run accident. That's all I remember. With the intense physical therapy, I was able to adapt to life in my wheelchair pretty quickly." She quickly changed the subject from the accident and smoothly transitioned to her love of science. "I think that's when I decided to face this new life and help others, which, as you know, led me to science and the healing of so many diseases. Also, since I just love animals, I made sure that in some way I would be able to help our Mammalia, or better stated, our creatures."

Russell looked around her living room and noticed how she proudly displayed her degrees, from her graduating from University of Marine Sciences as a lab technologist to her PhD in cytotechnology. "How did you expand your education from where you started to where you are now? And how would you explain to upcoming students what would be involved in the progression of studies?"

"You know, it's a different world once you enter the microscope. Our team faced challenges, but rewards were right behind. As I said before, science is inborn. It begins at a young age and develops over time. Cytotechnologists must expand in education if a student wishes to continue to help with all forms of life. Traditionally, testing in the cytopathology lab centers on screening for diagnosing diseases. Today, molecular testing can also influence treatment and prognosis." She silently exhaled her nervousness.

"As I look around your room, I see all the framed degrees proving the hard work in studies you accomplished and that you have earned your PhD. Share with me some of your discoveries that were published in the April issue in the *Science* journal." He placed his pencil at his chin as he watched in awe, her witty conversation distracting him from any thoughts of the wheelchair.

"Well, if it weren't for my team, who tirelessly works with me, I don't think I would have excelled as quickly. We found a mutated protein in a human cell and replaced it with human cell tissue of a healthy cell. When fused together, the healthy tissue actually grafted over the mutated cell and became clean again. This was a major breakthrough for one of our discoveries, which gave us many reasons to celebrate." Heather then leaned forward with a beaming smile.

"One more question, if you don't mind."

She knew what was coming next.

"Have you ever felt or thought that you might be able to find a way to help others to walk again? I know you have overcome this challenge by acceptance, but is there a chance to find a method of curing whatever would hold back anyone, including yourself, from recovering from a spinal cord injury?"

He sat back in the chair and crossed his legs while resting his finger on his jaw. He saw her uneasiness. She became tense, and her eyes shifted to the front door, then back to him almost a silent way of saying, "Leave now."

"At the age of ten, I was forced to live life as a paraplegic. Although I'm thankful that I can use my body from the torso up, I still face the fact that the wheelchair is my life. But I have to say I have found healing through my faith to go on. I think that is how I was able to go through school and move on to a higher education. Saying that, I believe there have been many scientists who are endlessly trying to repair this injury I have sustained. New scientific studies are conducted every day, and I believe there will be a cure in the very near future."

She felt a rush of blood throbbing through her body. She wanted to stand, but her legs were heavy and dead. Her body was shaky, and she managed to blink back the blurriness in her eyes. She faked a smile with the little of brain power she thought she had left and tried masking her nervousness.

Just as she wished it were over, he said, "Dear Heather, I thank you for all this time you have spent with me for this interview. This was a tremendous time for learning more about you and the wonders of science. I'll get back to you when I am finished with my story. It will take a while before it's actually published, but you will get a copy as soon as it hits newsstands."

He rose from his chair, shook her hand, and made his way to the door. Then he looked back. "Thank you again,

Heather. You are truly an awesome person. Good things will come your way very soon."

Heather was glad to see him go. She was exhausted from the interview. All his questions kept spinning through her mind. She thought, *Why did I even bother with this? It's not like I'm a celebrity. All those discoveries are really personal to me. I really don't like the question he asked me about spinal cord injuries. I felt a little taken back by it. Does he even know what it's like to live almost your entire life in a wheelchair? What does he think that a surgeon will suddenly come out of nowhere and bring a miracle cure for spinal injuries? I'm glad this is over. I can't wait to get to work tomorrow.*

It suddenly dawned on her that she should call her parents to tell them of the interview. She knew they would want to know. They would be so excited and proud. They had been with her every step of the way in her life.

"Hi, Dad. I have to tell you and Mom something exciting. I was just interviewed by the *New York Times*! How crazy is that?"

She held the phone steady and could hear the sound of his breath as he took in the surprise.

"Heather, my baby girl, this is beyond our wildest dreams. The *New York Times*? Wow, this is sensational. When can we buy it? When will it be published? How did this happen?"

His questions continued with electricity. She could feel it from the other end of the phone. Then she heard her mother's voice in the background. "What's going on? Come on, Richard, give me the phone...Heather, did I hear correctly? You were interviewed? Oh, my goodness. Well, you deserve this exposure for all that you do. Your father here is jumping like a child jumping rope. Honey, this is another calling card of adventure for you. I can't express how proud we are of you, how much we love you."

Heather could feel the tears of joy from her parents and their loving touch as if they were coming through the phone. "Mom, I'm hugging you back. I can't wait to see you again."

They couldn't feel her squeezing them back or see the grin that stretched across her face, but they knew what she felt, in that same way they could feel that family closeness to one another. *This is all quite astonishing for me, like peeking over the horizon and seeing my future ascending. This is what I needed. I understand why I worked so hard. This is my reward,* Heather thought.

Finally, after feeling drained, she got herself in her bed and cuddled up to her blanket. Slumber came like a soothing ocean breeze, bringing her deep into the arms of beautiful sleep.

After a couple of weeks, she did receive the copy that Russell had promised her. She carefully opened the large brown envelope and thought, *Well, I'm not on the front page. Let me see what page his article is on. Wow, I'm on the second page! That's almost on the front. It's quite a long story. I have to call Mom and Dad, then I'll bring it over to Jill's. What a writer. This is amazing!*

She went to visit Jill with the newspaper. Her eyes were alight as she spoke to her. "Jill, every muscle in my body feels like it wants to move, jump. I can't bottle up these feelings."

Jill laughed at the sight of how wide her friend's smile was and how she could light up the day with this exciting moment. She gave her the biggest hug.

"I think back to when we were in junior high when we were just children. I remember how we would giggle over such silly things. Everything was funny. But we had the best teachers, and we got our work done. It all paid off. You believed in your heart that you could be a champion. You owned it. You made it yours."

Heather felt strong. She had a feeling of self-worth. She had achieved a victory.

Chapter 13
The Gathering

Heather sat at her lab desk to begin her work. A couple of weeks had passed since the interview had been published. She listened to the rain with its steady patter dropping onto the glass skylight.

She thought as she leaned against her arm, looking upward, *There's a song in the rain. If I listen more intently, I can find it. But then again, it's just another morning without the sun's rays, like that morning of the accident. Lately, I just can't remove it from my thoughts. Even after that great interview, this memory still remains.* Her eyes followed down to the end of the long laboratory desk, and she thought, *I'm the height of a child in this wheelchair: forty-two inches for a five-year-old. If I could stand on my legs, what would my height be?*

She leaned on the desk, holding her head in her hands. *I'm wrapped in a cloak of despair; it's been years that I have hidden it. Only my heart knows how I wish to walk and dance and feel human, like when I was ten. What happened, Lord? Did you forget me?*

In her clouded thoughts, she heard the voices and footsteps of the team arrive. She quickly turned off her thoughts and greeted them. They were excited to begin their research using new plasma screens for detecting abnormalities in DNA, so they began to set up their desks and quickly went to work.

Dr. Harris made her daily check on the new recruits, then spoke to Heather.

"Heather, did you read the latest article about all your ambitious new discoveries that was published in the *New York Times* this week? I am so proud of you and everyone here as well. You are a fine example to these young interns. I placed the newspaper on a stand at the front desk for all to see. Besides becoming famous, you added some life to our laboratory. Also, I received a call from our local hospital, requesting a visit by their group of interns, accompanied by the lead surgeon. They like what they have read about our work-study program, specifically your studies and the results they have brought in the scientific study of splicing DNA. They were especially excited about meeting you and discussing your interview. We could use a little more glory here, don't you think?"

"Yes, Dr. Harris, I agree. We sure could use a little fame around here!" she said with a smirk and a giggle.

"Well, next Monday morning, they will arrive early, about 9 a.m. They requested to work with us for a few weeks since they are working on many injuries and diseases. This should be very interesting and will generate more vital information for doctors and patients of our endeavor to heal so many diseases."

With a smile, Heather agreed and looked forward to meeting doctors interested in her work and the success of the laboratory. The day passed quickly, and she couldn't wait to get home and call her parents again about more exciting news.

***

A week had passed, and the Monday morning for the doctors' visit arrived. Heather's eyes sparkled with anticipation in meeting the doctors and having an interview with them. Everyone was in their best attire, waiting for their visit.

Against the soft hum of the centrifuge in the background of the lab, everyone could hear Dr. Harris talking to the visiting doctors. The white-coated scientists stopped their work in the tissue culture room and moved in silence to the connecting office space just outside the laboratory.

Dr. Harris said, "Good morning, team. I would like you to meet our visitors."

One by one, Dr. Harris introduced each member of her team. After all were introduced with handshakes and light laughter; she then turned to Heather. "Dr. Storm, this is Dr. Ferris, the lead surgeon. Dr. Ferris, Dr. Storm is our cytogeneticist."

As he moved closer and extended his hand, their fingers touched. Heather was thunderstruck. It felt like their souls had been stirred. It was like a warmth of calmness, yet a feeling of oneness. She grasped her wheelchair, hoping to conceal her emotions. He was handsome, from the depth of his dark-brown eyes to his gentle expression in his speech.

He is so tall and so thin, she thought. *I love his dark, thick hair and his matching coffee-colored eyes. Why do I feel like I know him?*

Dr. Ferris said, "Ah yes, I finally get to meet the renowned doctor. The article in the *New York Times* really went into detail about your life. The most important factor was your passion to find an answer that is most needed. Your curious soul prepared the way for biological discoveries. I am so honored to meet you, Dr. Storm."

His voice quickened when he saw the glimmer in Heather's green eyes. For a moment, he forgot he was standing with his colleagues. Then he thought, *I feel like I already know her. Maybe it's from all the articles I've read about her.*

"Well, thank you, and I'm so glad to meet the highly regarded surgeon. Dr. Harris filled me in on your help with those in need in Wadala, Mumbai."

Their conversation was much more than words. It contained smiles and gentle shrugs while their eyes shone. They were both elated by each other's presence as they talked about their calling card of adventure in their professions. They shared the great challenges they had experienced. They both felt a strong sense of attachment to each other, a feeling of oneness. Their laughter filled the room until a team member interrupted.

"Excuse me, Dr. Storm, there seems to be a glitch in one of the thermal cyclers. I can't finish the extraction."

"Dr. Ferris, please excuse me. Let me just fix this problem. I'll be right back."

She quickly rolled herself to the other side of the room and began working with her assistant. The intern looked on and studied each movement she made. Each intern followed one of the technicians to their desks, and everyone returned to work. The interns were amazed at the new equipment that was being used. The doctors' and technicians' chatter brimmed over in the lab and synchronized with the humming centrifuge.

Heather returned to her desk to find Dr. Ferris inspecting some of her work. He was intensely absorbed in her scientific methods. "I have to say, this scanning tunneling microscope is giving a great view of changes through the process of mutation!" He was elated by the detail she had gathered. Heather smiled as her cheeks changed to a champagne pink.

The day moved quickly while they were immersed in work. Both doctors studied the observations and predictions, and again, they were interrupted by a team member.

"Hey, team, it's been a very long day for our first day together. What do you say we all get together and go for drinks tonight? We need to get to know one another since we will be working side by side for the next couple of months. What do you think?"

Dr. Frank looked at Jill, then casually leaned and rested his arm on her shoulder. She returned a sly look to him, and with a giggle, she yelled, "Yes!"

"Sounds great! I'll call ahead for reservations. A table for, let's see, how many?" The team member pointed to each person, counting and laughing. "Fifteen of us. I'll call now."

That night, they all met at the local café for a table of fifteen. Heather and Jill were already seated at the table waiting when they noticed their coworkers, who were like fish trying to swim through the large crowd in the busy café. Then Dr. Ferris quickly took the empty seat next to Heather.

John gave Jill a little grin from the side of his mouth. "Excuse me, I see an empty seat near you, Jill. Is it taken?"

"I don't see why not, Dr. Frank. We didn't finish our conversation this morning. What did you think?"

"I would like to see all your technical paperwork. I heard your office is filled with information the lab technicians filed with you."

Jill blinked her long, dark eyelashes at him and his bouncy body language. "Sure, it is really interesting to read daily reports on their findings. I could show you the DNA coding sequence that is broken down from their discoveries." She rested her elbows on the table and cupped her chin in her hands, staring into his eyes.

Meanwhile, Dr. Ferris was mesmerized by Heather's eyes. While he spoke to her, he could not move. He felt like his body was suddenly frozen in time. He said, "Well, we can actually all get to know one another this way since we will be troubling you with questions. Hope we don't get to be a nuisance." He ducked as the waiter brought a bounty of appetizers and drinks.

Heather's face blushed as she listened to him. "Oh, not at all. Actually, we feel handpicked. And it gives us a chance to hear more of the type of top-quality surgeries you've provided, Dr. Ferris."

"Well, first of all, just call me Robert. We are at ease here." The dim light of their surroundings couldn't hide his wide smile, and, in her mind, she repeated, *Robert*.

"Well, glad to meet you again, Dr. Ferris—I mean, Robert. Please just call me Heather." She gave a light, silly laugh.

It was the first time he had heard her first name; she had been introduced to him as Dr. Storm, and he had never thought about her first name. Her green eyes and her red hair attracted him, but now hearing the name of Heather gave him an emotion he had never felt before. He thought, *Heather. Just like the Heather from the beach. So strange to meet someone sharing the same resemblance and name except for the wheelchair.* There was a warmth in his heart, but he managed to shrug it off and continue the conversation. He went on to share his experiences in Moscow under the direction of Dr. Brezukaev and how he felt called to travel to Wadala, Mumbai. The other doctors also talked about their travels across the globe.

The night was about to end when Robert suggested that although it was late and time to leave, they should reunite at the end of the week.

"Aye!" John said. "All in favor?" As he jokingly tipped back his chair, he made eye contact with Jill. *I love looking into her deep-blue eyes,* he thought.

Jill spoke up, amused, and giggled at the doctor's carefree personality. "All votes in, it's a yes! How's Friday night?"

They departed the café and went separate ways. Jill took a car ride home with Heather, and as Jill stepped out of the car, she hesitated, then said, "Heather, you seemed to really connect with Dr. Ferris. Do you like him?"

A warm blush glowed across Heather's face at the unexpected question.

"Oh, Jill, come on now. It was just work-related conversations."

"It's just because you had so much to talk about, and you just met." Jill with a humorous banter elevating her question.

"Why are you questioning me like this? Look who's talking. I saw the way you and Dr. Frank swayed back and forth while you talked in the lab. And just now at the restaurant, I thought I saw sparks flying around you."

They both laughed, hysterical.

"So just stop and go home. I'll see you in the morning," Heather said as she looked up at Jill with a wide smile.

Heather got ready for bed. She pulled up the covers and started thinking.

I enjoyed my conversations with Dr. Ferris—I mean, Robert. It was a nice change from talking to the team at work. Somehow, it was different. Was it his eyes? It's like there's something hidden deep inside his dark eyes. He could be a really good friend to me. I don't think he would ever think of anything else, like a date with me and Mr. Steel.

Chapter 14
Shared Secrets

In the following weeks, the doctors worked closely with the laboratory pathologists. They paid special attention to Heather's gene splicing.

One of the new interns said, nearly holding his breath as he kept watching her intense work, "Dr. Storm, it is amazing to see how you extract the coding to separate it for analyzing. You have a keen eye and swift hand."

She looked up and gave a sweet smile. "Glad you're enjoying this. Now watch as I take this sample of tissue for results. If you think you're ready, you can do the next one."

A call came from the other side of the room as one of the interns, Adam, found something he wanted to share. "Heather, I'd like you to see this!" He waved her over. "By examining and testing this tissue, I found that it can help in the cause and nature of a connecting tissue that can be used during surgery. I followed one of your theories and found this to be true. What do you think?" Adam's tone of voice became robust as he waited for her reaction.

Heather took a long look through the microscope, then sat back and held out her hand to him.

"I love to see your success and thank you for studying my research and applying it to your work. I'm proud of you." Her firm handshake was an approval of his hard work.

Each day brought new discoveries with human tissue and genomic and proteomic biomarkers. Everyone in the lab worked on their interpretation of them, providing information for the treatment of patients. It was a new world for new pathologists.

One day, Dr. Harris called a special meeting for all to attend at the end of the day, saying, "Our speaker, Dr. Ferris, would like to address his team and, of course, my team on the subject of how surgeons work with pathologists and microbiologists."

Robert stood tall as he spoke about the relationship between surgeon and pathologist. He walked and talked with a refined delicacy. He was artful in his gestures and tactful with his words.

"The surgeon–pathologist relationship is an incredibly important aspect of the surgical care process. Everything is changing for pathology and the role of surgeons. This leads to better treatment options for our patients and to ensure the highest standard of safety and care. The findings of the pathologist after our spinal surgery can confirm that the appropriate course of action was taken. There are things that only the surgeon knows, and there are things that only the pathologist knows. If we bind those two together, we will see a dramatic increase in accuracy for the patient, which is our goal."

When his lecture was done, he walked to Dr. Harris to get some feedback and to make sure his audience had been engaged. Heather watched him closely. Her eyes followed his every gesture. The softness of his eyes gave her a warm sweetness to her soul. She'd never felt this before. There was a magic in the air. She could feel her youth again. There was an unusual scent, like the waves of the ocean passing by her. She would stare blankly, no matter what was happening in the room. She dropped her gaze to control her feelings.

After the meeting, all went back to their positions at their desks. Heather noticed Robert walking toward her, so she quickly flipped her hair behind her ears, letting the long waves bounce down her back. She pulled back her shoulders in a straight line, making herself a little taller, and she smiled.

"Hi, Dr. Storm. I was wondering, would you like to go to dinner with me one night? We need to talk more about the recent work you have accomplished. For the past few weeks, every time we've gotten together with the group, there's been so much talking, I can't get a word in." He gave her a broad smile as he held on to his notes and his eyes examined her face, waiting for her answer.

Her cheeks gave away her nervousness as she stammered out her words. "Oh, D-d-dr. F-f-ferris…um, y-y-yes, that would be great! I…I w-w-would love to have dinner with you. There's so much to t-t-talk about. Oh, okay, just give me the date and time. Will it be at the café? Did you say tonight? Do you have any suggestions?"

"There is another restaurant in the area. It's a little quieter than the café. I'll text you the address. Meet me there this Friday night at 6:30 p.m. if that's okay with you. Let me know when you're on your way so we can meet at the same time." With a wink to her, he turned and left the room.

Heather turned around to lean on her desk. She thought, *Oh, how I hope this heat in my face wasn't a giveaway about my excitement and nervousness. Is this a date? Couldn't be. It's about our work. He wouldn't be interested in a date with a wheelchair. I'm letting my emotions get out of hand. I can't stop my racing heart whenever I'm near him. I hope he doesn't notice. I think this is just a schoolgirl crush.*

Friday night finally arrived, and Heather was ready. It was 6:00 p.m., and she was about to text Robert when a text came through from him, letting her know he was ready to leave. She answered and said she was on her way. Heather was happy to have invested in her modified Honda. It had a mechanism to open the doors and lower a ramp. It was easy for her to lock her wheelchair to the floor and drive. It had given her much freedom.

He was waiting for her in the parking lot. He waved her over to park right next to him. He walked with her into the restaurant with pleasant conversation. They were seated at a little round table draped with a white tablecloth that reached the floor. In the center was a glowing red lamp. They sat close where they could feel the heat from the lamp.

"Well, Dr. Ferris...I mean, Robert," she giggled softly, "you really found a beautiful place for dinner. I had no idea that it even existed." Her face was enhanced by the glow of the lamp, adding sparkles to her emerald eyes.

"Dr. Storm—I mean, Heather," Robert said and winked, "you're so absorbed in all the details of your job, you probably don't even have time to find a place like this. So here you are. Now let's enjoy."

She watched him as he spread the avocado appetizer over some toast. "Mmm, you look like you're decorating a cake," she said with a subtle smile and a soft gaze into his eyes.

For the first time, he realized she was giving him all her attention, and for a moment, he felt absorbed by her smile and her playful words. As he placed the appetizer down, his hand brushed against hers. Was it the lamp or his own feelings that gave him a flash of warmth at that moment?

The tone of his voice rose a little higher in pitch. "Heather, has anyone ever told you that you have the most unusual green eyes?"

She felt the movement of his hand and, with prolonged eye contact, began to move her hair back over her ear. "Yes, I have, but coming from you, it sounds nicer." She began fidgeting with a button on her blouse.

He moved in closer. "You're a very interesting girl. We've never talked about your life. Where did you say you lived?" His question was burning with curiosity.

"Well, we can get to that next. I'm just as curious about you as you are about me. So tell me, Mr. Secret Man, where do you actually live? I mean, you've lived all over the world, but where is your home?"

"I was born and raised in Glen Cove, Long Island. Graduated high school there and left for Russia. My mom said I was very mature for my age and knew I would be fine out there. Now all these years later, I feel I have really lived my life. Even though I'm in my thirties, I feel much older." His laughter released some of the tension he felt, but at the same time, he couldn't take his eyes off her glowing face.

"New York! The busiest place to live, don't you think? I'm a Jersey girl from Point Pleasant. But my parents wanted to retire to Florida, so after I graduated high school, they moved to Florida and I was able to get my degree at the University of Marine Sciences, then I followed my desire to work in the lab. After all that and a few years later, I found an opening right here in New York, so here I am!" Laughing, she spread her arms wide.

"Well, what about your parents? Do they want to remain in Florida?" he asked.

"I think eventually they'll move back to New Jersey. We own a cottage in Holgate, and I think they miss it. I would be surprised if they didn't come back. My father said he misses the change of the seasons, and Mom is complaining it's always hot, so I think it will be soon."

Robert jumped as she said the name of the town. *Holgate?* he thought. *It has to be the same little town where my parents took me each summer.* "Holgate? Wait— Holgate, the little New Jersey beach town?"

"Why, yes. It's a famous town for the summer. All the families go there. That's why it sounds familiar to you," she said as she bushed it off, not realizing there was more to it than just the name of this town.

Robert listened to her and realized she could be right about Holgate, so he just continued on with the conversation. "I can understand that. I would miss the different seasons also, especially the snow! Also, I am amazed at your creativity. It looks like magic when you're at work." He was leaning a little more toward her, with his elbows resting on the table and one hand grasping his chin.

"I have to say, I feel like a writer when I'm making changes to the DNA strands. I spend so much time alone, just me and my ideas in a creative bubble. Yet there are days I need other people around. That's why I really appreciated when you came to our lab and we all started going out to the café. It's great to be able to emerge from my desk!" She laughed as if it were a natural spring flowing from her.

Their first date brought up so many emotions as they talked and shared about their lives and jobs, they both had good feelings about each other. The night went smooth as a couple of hours flew by. At the end of the evening, he walked her to her car and watched her enter with ease. As they said their goodbyes, their eyes held a deep gaze and both felt a chemistry connection.

***

Their conversations helped them know more about each other, and they developed a strong friendship. The weeks went by as they worked together, researching more about spinal cord tissue transplants, and they continued their dinners, not realizing their flirtatious actions were increasing as they talked about their lab experiences and updates on their findings.

At times while Heather was busy at her desk, Robert would sit close to her with his arm around the back of her chair and observe and interact with her sampling of tissue. She would feel the heat rise in her face at the mere touch of his arm resting on her back. She would look up at him, and their eyes would lock in a moment.

Their dinners became more frequent at the same cozy restaurant. The owner would greet them each time they arrived and give them the same small, round table in the back. He knew their usual order and always had their favorite bottle of wine ready for them.

"Robert, I'm so glad you picked this place; the atmosphere is dreamlike. I love the vintage collection of chairs and tables. And the stained-glass Tiffany lamps are like heirlooms. I feel like I'm sitting in a treasure box." She reached over and took his hand and gave it a soft squeeze.

"This is our place. I feel like I own it! I'd rather come here with only you." His genuine feelings for her were conveyed in his words, followed by a return squeeze of his hand on hers as he gazed longingly into her eyes. There was a deepening of their feelings for each other with each evening they spent together. It was a new relationship as in a new day for them. Heather felt a fresh start in her life and a new joy in her heart.

***

During the following week, Heather thought, *It's been so long since Jill and I have had some quality time alone, some girl time. I have so much to share with her.* So she gave her a call that night and set a date and time to go together to a quiet restaurant.

"I'm so glad you decided on a girls' night out. I mean, we speak at work and always on the phone, but we need this special time to regroup in so many ways. I kind of thought you were much too busy with Robert—I mean, Dr. Ferris—to have a dinner with me," Jill said with a happy but inquisitive smile as she swirled her wine around in its glass.

"Of course, Jill. I've been thinking about this for weeks. But let's skip Robert for a moment. I want to know all about this doctor you've been seeing, Dr. Frank? I wanted to ask you how it's going now that you have been out a few times.

I like him. He's cute and really direct with his work," Heather said, prying for information.

Jill flipped her curled hair and fluttered her lashes as she giggled like a child. "Oh, Heather, he is great! Call him John. He is so thoughtful. He always asks me how I'm doing. Calls and checks up on me. He shows me that he genuinely cares about me. Now he's sending me little cards in the mail. He even leaves a red rose on my desk! We really get along like best friends...sorry, old friend, you're really my bestie, but he treats me like a queen. And did you know that he and your Robert are best friends?"

"You're still hysterical, and I'm glad it's going so well for you. Yes, I do know that they studied in Moscow together. Then Robert was called home because of his father's illness, so that separated their friendship for a while. But look at them now, they are like brothers. Now, thinking back to our first couple of years in college in Florida, do you remember that guy who was studying with you, but you said he loved the beaker more than you?"

Jill still had a twinkle in her eyes. "Ha, yes, that was such a waste of time. Wonder what he's doing now? He's probably still engaged to the beaker. I'm so glad I moved on. Who would have thought I would meet such a great man like John?"

"So, tell me about the first kiss! Come on now, tell me!" Heather prodded with her girlish laugh.

Jill's hands shook with excitement like a child. "Yes, but not just the first kiss. There were many after that one! He hinted to me that he would like to take me to his hometown and meet his parents. I know this is it. This is the one I've been waiting for. My life is so full now. I'm so happy!" Jill's deep-blue eyes showed her excitement.

Heather said, "Well, my dear old friend, I feel a wedding coming in the extremely near future. Let's toast to it!"

They raised their glasses to their future and to the anticipated announcement of a wedding.

***

One night, Heather was working late. All the interns and pathologists had left. She sat alone finishing up when Robert walked in.

"Dr. Storm—Heather, my friend—I've brought you a cup of coffee. Let's just stop all this work and relax a little." He handed her the coffee and sat next to her. His thick, black eyelashes blinked as he looked at her, and he felt such a strong emotion that he had to turn his head away for a moment.

"Well, thank you, Dr. Ferris—I mean, Robert, my friend." She giggled at the joke they always said to each other. "This is nice, just relaxing. But you look troubled." She shifted toward him, sipping her coffee.

Cove had been thinking about their last conversation about the beach town of Holgate; he became more curious.

"A long time ago, I met a little girl at the beach. I must have been only ten at the time. But she has remained on my mind all these years. It was a special time in my life. You remind me of her, not only because you have the same name but there is a strange resemblance." He stared at her in wonder.

173

"Her name was Heather? She had this color of red hair? What a coincidence." She sat puzzled as she pulled some of her hair into a twist.

"Well, with your name being the same, your green eyes, and your red hair, you do resemble her. But that was so many years ago." He sat still and up straight, focused intently on what her answer might be.

Heather slowly placed her coffee down on the desk. She caught the scent of an ocean, a vision of soft sand, a recollection of a time from long ago.

"Robert, you mentioned a beach. Did you ever vacation at a family beach down in South Jersey? It's called Holgate Beach."

"Yes, you mentioned that at our first dinner. It stirred a memory. My parents would take me there for a couple of weeks at a time during the summer. I can't believe it. You were there too? Could it be we were there at the same time?" His eyes blazed with questions as he steadily gazed at her.

Heather was not quite smiling and had to catch her breath as she spoke. "Robert, I have to tell you, I wasn't always in this wheelchair. I was once a little girl who played on the beach and swam. I ran with long legs like a ballerina to the shore and picked up shells. I was very much alive. Then one day that was filled with a dark haze, I was in an accident, which left me paralyzed. I could have been on that beach with you. Maybe we did play in the sand together. We just wouldn't know that now since we have matured and physically changed."

His words forcefully spilled out as he stared at her with sizzling interest. "Wait a minute, Heather. Did you meet a boy by the name of Cove at any time at that beach?"

Heather's eyes lit up like the burning sun. Her mouth opened in the shape of a circle. "Why, yes. How did you know something like that? Yes, I did, when I was ten."

At that moment, her words stopped, and her heart leaped. Her lips couldn't move, and she couldn't breathe, as if underwater. She lifted a shaky finger and pointed to him.

"You know him! Wait…could it be you?" Her eyes widened, desperately searching his face for an answer.

"Heather, my nickname is Cove. Only my close friends call me that. I'm the Cove you met when we were ten. And I can prove it. I have half of something, and you have the other half."

He reached over and began to gently stroke her hands as the shock registered on her face. Then like a cloud burst over her head, there was a vivid image of the time they had spent on that hot, summer day.

"The shell! Yes, I have a half shell. You have the other half? How could this be? After all these years. How did you know it was me? Oh my goodness, is this real? I feel like I'm in a fantasy." Her words became shaky, and every muscle in her body just froze. Then a grin crept onto her face. Her smile stretched from one side to the other.

He grabbed her hand and held it tightly. "Well, at first, the name Heather just clicked in my mind. But when I saw your eyes, I felt a connection. Honestly, the wheelchair threw me off. As I got to know you, I had a deep feeling it was you. I've never stopped thinking of you. I feel like we were supposed to meet again. I just don't know why."

Heather's questions poured out like a fountain as her excitement heightened. "Did you look for me after our first meeting? Did you ever go back to find me?"

"My parents purposely took another week of vacation two weeks after that so I could. I always searched for you until the summer was over."

"Cove, didn't you hear any rumors of an accident?"

"No, I had no idea. If we had, we probably would have rushed to the hospital and inquired about it. I wish I had heard something at that time. But look at this—we are together again." Cove couldn't take his eyes off her. He was still in disbelief that he had found her.

Heather's eyes gleamed as her face grew brighter. "Do you remember how you tried to open that shell? It was so stuck together. Then finally, with your long fingers and a stick, you pulled it apart. I'll never forget how shiny it was. I can see how you're a highly skilled surgeon with those long, slim fingers."

He felt a boyish grin cover his face just like when he had first given her the other half of the shell. "I do remember. How could I forget the struggle to get that shell open? And you thought there would be a pearl inside. If there were, I would have given it to you."

"That was what you said to me when I asked if there was a pearl inside." The muscles in her face became relaxed. She became quiet with a serious expression. The memory became real.

They talked for hours, erasing all the questions they had held on to for all those years, finally finding the answers about their disappearances. There was a rekindling of their souls. Their love was like a comforting blanket wrapped around them. What was lost had now been found.

Chapter 15
A Short Retreat

From then on, they spent every moment possible together. Their laughter became like a soundtrack of their souls. Their weekends were overflowing wherever they were, at work or their dinners, allowing them to share their remembrances of that play day on the sand. *Her laughter is so free and pure, almost childish, despite her adult years, just like when we were kids*, Cove thought.

One night, Cove couldn't sleep. Everything about her stayed on his mind: the beauty of her eyes, the shimmer in her hair, and especially her laughter, a special kind of laugh that filled his soul with joy. He was amazed at how she could laugh so much and put aside her disability. Even though she remained in a wheelchair, it showed him how she could put others at ease and hide her own emotions. It all amazed him how she had pulled together enough strength to follow her career. He was deeply in love with her. Cove felt he was very serious with Heather and wanted to take her to meet his parents, but he thought he should explain her condition to them first. It was a Saturday night when he went for dinner at his parents'. It was during dessert time that he began to explain.

"Mom, Dad, I need to talk to you about something very serious." He held his breath for a second and released with a sound.

"Cove, what could be so serious? Please just tell us." Mary stopped serving dessert and sat down in silence.

"I met someone, she's bright, funny, and beautiful. I met her at the laboratory where I went with my team. She studies cells and DNA. I'm in love with her. And I want you to meet her." He waited, his stomach turning like a roller coaster.

"Well, is that what this is about, for a minute there I was afraid of something disastrous. Tell us more about her, this is wonderful." Joseph sat back relieved and ready to listen.

"Well besides all the beauty she attains and the fun we have together, she has been in a wheelchair since she was ten. But there's more. We recently found why we are so connected. She was the little girl I met on the beach. Do you remember now?" Cove sat as an adrenaline surge filled his body.

"Oh, yes, you called her Heather and you two found a shell, yes, I distinctly remember. You couldn't find her before we left. Well after all these years, I'm amazed at this story." Mary was stunned, and she felt emotional pressure.

They talked for hours, reminiscing about that time at Holgate beach. The search Joseph did before they left. Cove explained about the hit and run that made Heather paralyzed. He explained how independent she was and how she had accomplished so much in her life. He expressed what a miracle it is that after years of thinking of her she's back in his life.

"Well, son, it sounds like she was supposed to be in your life. And if you think that you can live with all that comes with a life in a wheelchair, then of course we bless your decision. Bring her here, we have to meet her. It will be great to talk about our favorite vacation spot." Joseph felt a sense of calmness about Cove's decision. Then Mary leaned over to her son and reached for his hand to show him she agreed.

The following week Cove and Heather were on their way to meet his parents. It was a pleasurable time spent with Mary and Joseph. While reminiscing how Cove and Heather met at Holgate beach and all the fun time they had playing in the sand, they also could hear her emotional pain that flowed out from her heart in her words. Mary and Joseph listened intently as Heather described all the physical therapy she went through and having to yield to her wheelchair. They felt the sadness as they pictured her life and opened their soul to her. The evening was filled with a welcome to Heather, filled with moments of tears, laughter, and a fresh page for them all that kindled something beautiful within them.

When Heather returned home, she called Jill and invited her to come over. She needed to tell her of this new romantic event in her life. Jill arrived and they sat in her living room, drinking tea and some cookies.

"Well, now it's your turn to tell me about your visit with Robert's parents, all the juicy stuff." Jill rubbed her hands together in anticipation.

"Jill, it was like meeting old friends. It was divine pleasure, chatting with old friends, reminiscing about our past, and we developed a sweet bond of family. They accepted me and Mr. Steel. Oh Jill, I just can't believe it. When he drove me home, before he helped me out of the car, he held me ever so tightly, and then his kiss was a kiss of deep love, the sweetness of passion all rolled into one."

Jill jumped up and danced around the room, then she grabbed a cookie and said, "Heather your life is now sweeter than this cookie. Looks like it's not just my wedding we are planning." She held Heather, and they both shared in a crying fest of joy.

***

Cove felt a deep desire to do more for her. He felt she was his companion, his best friend, his future wife, but more importantly, he felt his love for her was so strong that he had to help her. He knew he loved her the day he had met her when he was only ten years old. He knew he had been sent to her to help her, to be her surgeon. The desire was so deep in his heart, the same as the desire he had had to go to Wadala. He knew he was right about this decision too.

He made a call to a colleague at The Spine Hospital at Mount Sinai and discussed Heather's case. They met and talked about her condition and came to an agreement that a special surgery could be done with the new medical advancement that was available for spinal cord injuries. He hoped she would be willing to undergo testing.

Friday night was their usual night for trying different restaurants, searching for special cuisine that would quench their appetites. Cove decided to bring dinner to her apartment, because he didn't know how she would react to the suggestion of having surgery, so he wanted to ensure their privacy.

"Okay, Heather, I brought a special dinner. I thought this setting would be quieter where we could talk. I have here an assortment of cheeses. Brie is my favorite one. There are biscuits and the main course. You must try this aloo gobi. It's Indian cuisine, the most delicious cauliflower with potatoes and marsala wine." He nervously put down the packages of food.

"Sure, Cove, I set the living room coffee table for us with my crystal candleholders. Thought it would be cozier."

They enjoyed the new foods as they laughed and talked and felt such freedom with each other. Then Cove sat hushed for a while, trying to break his news to Heather.

"You know all about my research and surgeries from these past years. Well, I spoke with a few of my colleagues this week. I have great news for you. Even the chief neurosurgeon agrees that I could perform surgery on your injury. There have been such medical advancements, you could be healed—"

He waited for her reaction, hoping she would be thrilled with the news, but she stopped him as soon as she heard the word *healed*. She bit her inner lip, then held up her hand against his face to stop him.

"Don't say another word! Let me set you straight right now: I will never go through that again. After the accident, I lived in that hospital for almost a year. I went through traction upside down for seven weeks, then I had to live through all types of physical therapy. I'm lucky I can move from the waist up. No more hospitals, no more surgeries, no more therapies. It's done. I'm done!"

The anger from her eyes showed the scared child within, the little girl who had had to fight for her life. Cove could see the pain beneath it all and the weariness of her soul.

"Heather, please, believe me, I understand. I have been with patients who had to live in therapy for a year or more. I know what the surgery is like. I perform it; that's why I looked into it for you! Don't you realize this might be why we've been able to reconnect?"

Confusion boiled deep in his mind and heart. He felt darkness swallow him up as he watched her hold her head. Then she turned on him like an enraged panther.

"You only remember me with legs, running with you to the shore and back. You remember picking up seashells and filling up buckets. You only remember that little girl. I'm not that little girl anymore. Look! Look hard at me. You just can't let go of that memory. Maybe this is too much for you, watching me pull my body around in a wheelchair. Your memory of that little girl has been washed away like the ocean tide. Life was good then, but this is me now. If this is not good enough for you, just leave!"

With a hard stare at Cove and her face the color of an overripe tomato, she wheeled herself to the door, opened it, and gestured for him to leave. Awkwardly, Cove walked to the door. Then he stopped and turned to her.

"You're allowing that dark day to hover over you like that morning fog. It's clouding your judgment. Slay your dragons, Heather. I'll leave you alone. See you Monday morning."

With that, he left. He wasn't angry. He was low in spirit for thinking this would have made her happy. He thought, *I'll let her rest on this. I know we have met again for a reason. I have to keep my faith, and I believe it is for me to help her. She just doesn't know it yet.*

***

By Monday morning, Cove was hoping to find a speck of light in the dark lab and that Heather wouldn't shrug him off because of their last conversation. He stood in the doorway, watching her already busy as usual at her desk. His heart was filled with love for her. He just couldn't tell her yet. He moved slowly toward her, not knowing how to start the conversation. She felt something behind her, so she looked up and saw him standing over her.

"Well, good morning, Dr. Ferris. I would like you to examine this piece I just separated." Her gesture was as empty and cold as her words as she jerked her hand upward and pointed to the microscope.

After Cove examined the code, he agreed that her conclusion for understanding the structure and function of tissue she had reached of her study of this particular code was correct. He was still amazed at her ability to acquire and apply knowledge. As he gazed into her eyes, he saw a need for nurturing, and he thought, *All she needs is my love, something true to hold on to. How I can rescue her, rescue myself, if only she would let me?*

"Very good, Dr. Storm. My crew and I truly appreciate all that you have given to us these past weeks. We will take your study with us for our chief physician to review. We have finished up here and extend thanks to you and all your staff."

He quickly turned to leave without a backward glance to her. After a few days, he didn't call, he didn't text, he didn't email. He severed himself from the uncomfortable, complicated relationship, hoping that by being distant she would rethink their situation and call him.

***

Days, then weeks passed, with Heather's mind in shreds; she couldn't get that last picture of Cove out of her mind. The way he had turned and left, never looking back at her. Each time her eyes closed; she saw the same image of him.

Just then, Jill was at her door, ringing and knocking, calling her name. When Heather opened the door, Jill slowly walked in. Heather was relieved to see Jill; she wanted their friendship to express her feelings to her one true friend.

"Heather, it's been weeks, and I have watched you stay secluded here in your apartment. Other than work, you don't speak a word. I see the wall you've built between us. I've been your true friend for years. Why hide behind a wall of depression when you can speak to me? I can help you with all this."

Heather's tears burst forth like water from a dam. "I am so sorry, Jill. I've become like the recluse spider. I hate myself. I hate that I am here in this wheelchair. I fell in love with Cove. I never told him, and then I chased him away."

Her words quivered. Then she engulfed a large breath and exhaled. Jill could see the loss that had swept over

Heather's mind and body. She said, "Okay, let's talk this out. We can come to some kind of resolution."

They talked for a few hours, their conversation filled with tears, smiles, and a sense of peace in the arms of friendship. Jill was able to make sense of her friend's discomfort about the surgical procedure. As they talked, Heather remembered again how deep her love was for Cove and how Cove loved her so much he wanted to use his expertise to help her.

"Heather, you have to call him. It's time. Don't hide behind your emotions and the wheelchair. This could be your destiny. Cove was meant to come back into your life. He's a godsend." Jill sat back with a release of her breath, knowing what was going to happen, that Heather would listen to her.

"Oh, Jill, I have so many battle wounds from the life I've lived. I've been in so much emotional pain since he left that I know I should call him; I know we are in love. Now that I think of it, Cove has never mentioned Mr. Steel. Come to think of it, it's almost as if it's not even part of me. He sits so close to me with his arm around my shoulder. A little secret, Jill: he kissed me. It was a tender moment, like a burst of love he expressed, not caring and not feeling the cold steel around me. It was just me and Cove. And he whispered in my ear that there's a scent of floral bouquet around me. I felt his breath and it sent tingles through me. It was the beginning of a romance. How can I let that go? He loves me in this wheelchair! He just wants the best for me. Thank you for helping me to sort this all out. My mind was in such a stage of perplexity. I could not deal with or understand the whole idea that he presented to me. Now I'm thinking clearly. Please Jill, pray with me."

They held hands and prayed for guidance and wisdom. Then Heather felt herself fill with strength. Jill left feeling much had been accomplished during their talk and knew Heather and Cove's relationship would be mended. Heather then reached for her phone and called Cove.

"Cove, please, I'm so sorry. I felt like I had to defend myself. I have this power over me because I've always been the one to take care of myself, to make my own decisions. I'm a prisoner to my own beliefs. Clearly, I regret my actions toward you. I understand now that you want the best for me, you want me healed. Please come back to me."

It was a profound moment for them both, a moment of the gift of emotional healing, stamped with the seal of love.

***

In just a few days, she found herself at the restaurant, waiting for Cove. She sat watching from her seat alongside of the buffed glass of the long fish tank that sat in the center of the room. She admired how the different-colored fish could swim so smoothly. She thought, *Beneath those scales are a skeleton that's not even used for walking. Could I have a chance to use my legs to swim again one day, to walk, and to dance?* There was a melody to the way the fish swam. Her eyes followed as they circled around in the tank like a dance. Then she felt a warm touch on her shoulder.

Cove said, "Heather, I can't express what this means to me. I've waited all this time for you to call me. So many times, I began to call you, then stopped. The last time I left you, I thought you were done with me. Please believe me that I did not intend to hurt you." He slowly sat down, pulling the chair closer to her and steadily holding his breath, waiting for her to speak.

It was like the melancholy cloak she had been wearing for years had just fallen to the ground. All the emotional pain surfaced as she shared her deepest feelings. "Cove, it's not you, it's me. I've been hiding my feelings behind the shelter of a thick wall. All these years, I've pretended, through my laughter, to have made peace with my condition. It's all a cover-up. I've been drowning in my thoughts more and more each year. Sure, I joke that my best friend is Mr. Steel, but when I'm alone, I'm really alone."

"Listen to me, Heather: This is the beginning of a new life for you. All your suffering that you have hidden will now have to leave. I don't doubt why we were finally brought together. I know—I believe—that we were supposed to reconnect at this exact time. Just think, why in the world would we meet again after more than two decades? Why would I keep my half of the shell, and why was I led to become a spinal surgeon? The answer is fate."

Then he lifted something from his pocket and placed it on the table near her. Her eyes widened and lit up; her mouth quivered. Her delicate fingers reached over and picked up the shiny, pearlescent shell and brought it to her heart. She then moved the collar of her top to reveal her necklace with her half of the shell.

"Oh, Cove, you still held on to it. I always thought the other half had been lost. But now I see this half has brought us together. It's a match, like us."

She leaned forward, stretching out the necklace toward him. He lifted his half of the shell and matched it to hers. He was close enough to her that he could feel her heartbeat. He softly kissed her, a kiss that lasted a long time. Cove's fate was to rescue the only girl he could not dismiss from his memory. Their love was like that. It had become stronger, and now it was unstoppable.

***

Weeks passed, and Heather completed all of her presurgical assessments. The surgeon and surgical assessment team gathered the information and results to understand Heather's medical history. The evaluation included an in-depth review of her medical history and findings from X-rays, CT scans, MRI studies, and blood tests. The final test was a physical and neurological examination. Then her appointment was made for the doctor's review and explanation of the procedure, and, if she was a candidate, to set the date for the surgery.

All the reasons not to do this came flooding to her mind. She remembered the Stryker frame and how she had hated facing the floor and the nausea that had come over her when the nurses had turned her around. The muscle pain that had come with the physical therapy. And then the wheelchair that had permanently become part of her body. As a child, she had thought of it as extra legs. Her thoughts changed to hope as she met Cove at the office. He sat next to her with great anticipation, knowing his friend and chief surgeon would accept her for this new procedure.

Heather felt like a wound deep inside was about to swallow up all her hopes and dreams. "Cove, I feel a soft panic right now. I can't imagine what the results of all the tests have concluded."

"Heather, today could make the difference between you staying in Mr. Steel and walking with me arm in arm. You mean the world to me. You've worked so hard in changing and repairing the world with all your discoveries, now it's time for your life to change and for the world to give back to you." Cove felt hopeful and confident about her future. He gave her a shining smile and held her hand, comforting her with his words.

Dr. McGuiness finally arrived, carrying a white chart, and he sat behind his desk. His silver hair shone from the sunlight filtering through the window behind him. He made a slight sound as he precisely turned each page, then looked up with a smile.

"I'm sorry for mumbling out loud. I'm thinking deeply about all the test-related answers here in your chart. It is my mission to bring healing to my patients if they fit the criteria for this type of surgery."

The mood suddenly shifted; intense worry and a painful thought took over Heather's mind, hoping she did meet the criteria. A questioning look flashed on her face as she sat with her fingers tightly intertwined with Cove's.

"My dear, there has been a breakthrough in thoracic spine surgery, as Dr. Ferris must have explained to you. He is our top surgeon here, and his expertise is trustworthy. We have worked together for years on this modern diagnostic technology. The microsurgical technique has replaced the general surgical techniques. Dr. Ferris, you may interject here at any time." He leaned back in his chair, handing the chart over to Cove.

"Heather, you and I have discussed this before. That last article you read about robotic assistance in surgeries? Let's review it now. It helps us to navigate deep into the thoracic and lumbar part of the spinal cord, which will result in disability reduction. As a spinal cord surgeon, there is much more involved that I can't explain to you in layman's terms. But trust us in this procedure. I want to improve the quality of your life." Underneath his serious expression was a steady love for her and the hope that she understood not just the seriousness of the operation but the possibility of a new life for her.

"Thank you, Cove. I do understand since I work with DNA and tissue splicing, so I know what to expect. I also did some research on the new techniques. It is amazing that this can be done." At this time, she began to feel more confident. The chief surgeon said.

"Let me interject here, Heather, that the CT scans and the 3D radiograph, the MRI, and the Doppler ultrasound all show you are a great candidate for this particular surgery. Twenty years ago, this was not available, but you are living in a time of a medical breakthrough. There is nothing to worry about. You will have the best of care. Since I am the chief surgeon, Dr. Ferris will be assisting me, but of course, I will allow him to use his expertise in this area. Normally, surgeons don't operate on a loved one, but because of his existing proficiency, he will lead with me. Your outcome is written beyond this chart. Your faith is giving you the answer to trust in God. Even in your fear, trust us."

Faith had given Heather a step toward a stronger feeling of survival. It reminded her of the broken spirit and body she had felt for so long, and now she felt a renewal of body and mind.

A decision had been reached to end this competition between her spirit and her constant companion, Mr. Steel.

Chapter 16
Heaven's Healing

Time seemed to crawl for Heather. It had already been three weeks of waiting for her upcoming date for surgery. She marked her calendar in red. *It will be tomorrow,* she thought, *and my parents will meet me at the hospital. Everyone I love will be with me.*

Then, unexpectedly, Jill appeared at her door.

"Jill, what a surprise. You didn't call." Heather was trying to tie up her hair as she signaled Jill to sit with her.

"Heather, I felt I need to be here with you today to help you get ready for tomorrow. You have a big day ahead of you, and I don't want you to be all alone today. I know Cove has surgeries all day today and he can't stop by, so here I am!" Jill made a comical face with her palms outward as she gave a little giggle.

Heather rested her elbows on the rim of the steel armrest, just staring into Jill's soft, understanding eyes. "Oh, Jill, only you can take my mind off all this. I'll be okay. I know I fought this surgery for a while, not knowing that there had been an advancement in this type of spinal injury. After all the studies I have done, I wouldn't have known of this technique that Cove had learned while in

Russia with Dr. Brezukaev. I just find it so unreal. Sometimes when I'm with Cove I can still smell the ocean. That's how I know this was all orchestrated by God."

"Seriously, I'm here for the night. That sofa is very comfortable. I already made the arrangements with Cove to get you up at six a.m. and on the road to the hospital. It's all working out for you. This is the biggest moment of your life." Still being comical, Jill waved her arms to lighten the mood.

"You know, your personality very much matches John's. I'm glad you two met." Heather smiled a serious, loving smile.

"Oh yes, my life is really moving on with him. We have had some serious talks about how our lives have meshed so beautifully. We love the same things, like walking through Central Park or going to an art exhibit. We love the same music. He dedicates that song by Elton John to me; you know, the one called 'Your Song.' But I'm not here about that. I'm here to be with you through this whole surgery, from beginning to healing." Jill clasped her hands together in prayer and winked.

"Yes, and you have been along my life journey since we met. You're here now and will always be with me, I'm confident in that thought."

At the end of the evening, they bowed their heads together in prayer, believing all would go well tomorrow, that the anesthesia, the doctors, and the surgery would be blessed by God.

The next morning, Heather was prepped for surgery. As she lay there with the IV inserted into her arm, she peered into the bright light overhead. She thought to herself, *Here*

I am, looking upward into this bold light. It's like looking into the high beams of a car's headlights. I hope I don't have to wake up looking down into a cold, gray floor again. I can feel my heartbeat in my neck like a vacuum sucking in all my fears, taking in all my thoughts. Dear God, please let this go well. Let me be whole.

Cove walked in covered in green scrubs, ready for the surgery. He leaned toward her and held her hand.

"Heather, breathe deep. All will be fine. I'm here. I will always be here with you. I love you." Then he kissed her forehead.

Slowly, her eyes were closing. She could see Cove. Then he became clouded like shadows passing, eventually melting into darkness.

***

In the operating room, Cove looked up at the oversize clock that hung on the wall. It was 7:49 a.m. Then he looked at the chief surgeon.

"Are you ready to begin, Dr. Ferris? If so, make the first cut. I will follow after that."

"Yes, sir, I am ready. Scalpel, please."

As Cove began, with each incision, he felt the heat in his face. He knew this would be a complex surgery, but like a battle cry, his heart said it had to be done. He was the warrior who would defend his love.

When it was the chief surgeon's turn, he inserted the tubular retractor dilators, moving aside the muscles and creating a tunnel through the tissues down to the spinal column. He was a seasoned doctor, using his hands swiftly and precisely.

He spoke sternly through his mask, "I must say, Dr. Ferris, we are working in unison to achieve this mission for Heather's sake."

"Yes, Doctor, I see by the clock that time is moving swiftly. It's now 11:04 a.m. I feel good about this. I will now do the spinal fusion and graft bone tissue to form one solid bone. I already see the tissue meshing together like beautiful latticework."

Cove was now feeling more certain about the surgery. Then suddenly, the bone tissue stopped knitting together, and the nerve roots coming out of the spinal cord were now visible. Cove thought, *She has been under anesthesia long enough, I have to make another decision and move quickly. Did I push her too far into this surgery, was this the right idea?*

The chief surgeon said, "Dr. Ferris, you know the consequence of operating on the wrong vertebral level. Think now. What protocol would you use at this very moment to prevent it?"

"I have to line up the bony spinal column and add in one rod, which will retract the nerve roots and bring the tissue in so it wraps around the vertebra. I have to move fast."

Moisture dripped through the pores of his skin and lay on Cove's face. Every muscle felt tight. He swallowed hard and kept his eyes on Heather's spine. He thought, *This has to work, don't think negative, think positive.* He was oblivious to his surroundings. He was on the outside looking in and directing himself. There was just a buzzing sound around him as his adrenaline pumped and beat like it was trying to escape, but his hands didn't tremble. He was focused and in control for her, for his love.

Cove checked the clock. It was 1:11 p.m., and they completed the surgery. He watched as they rolled Heather into the recovery room. He felt this had been the worst experience of his life when he thought the surgery wasn't going as he planned, just the thought of the tissue not connecting. But he took a breath and remembered that he was expertly trained; he had been able to rectify what could have happened in the operating room. Then he met the chief surgeon in the changing room.

"I was waiting for you to come back, Dr. Ferris. I must say, this was one of my best surgeries, and I was accompanied by the best surgeon. You took quick action at a time where it could have been fatal. You were precise under stress. I am proud of you."

"This brings me to another subject. I will be retiring next year and will have to nominate my successor. I want my knowledge and experience to remain at this hospital for a long time. I see you are the one to continue in my shoes. We will discuss this more thoroughly at next week's board meeting." He grabbed Cove's shoulder, gave him a tight squeeze and a wide smile, and left.

Cove stood amazed, almost overwhelmed. Then, to his own surprise, he felt his lips stretch wider into an uncontrollable, gaping grin at the thought that he could be the next chief of spine surgery. But his thoughts quickly went back to Heather, the thought if he hadn't acted quickly, if he hadn't caught the loose vertebrae. He stopped the negative thinking and gave thanks to God for helping him to heal Heather, his love.

***

Was her consciousness swirling in a land of dreams? She blinked at the infinite hues of rippling white that formed into a lacy wedding dress. Then there was the sound of trumpets mixed with a soft touch of a piano melody that filled the air as the clouds drifted by. The glowing hues of colors formed a pattern covering like a ceiling of artwork the human eye had never seen before.

A golden ray passed through like a lightning bolt and opened the clouds, revealing two golden doors. A wind surged through them, carrying heavenly white doves with brilliant rays shooting out from their wings. Their bodies soared across the clouds' silver linings and circled back.

The ground was crystal, clear as glass, winding in an upward staircase that led to a white throne with rays in golden hues shooting out and framing its arched back. The throne was covered in sapphires and rubies. Their colors formed an arc like outstretched hands above the chair, the brilliance so vivid it was almost blinding. A golden lion sat at each side of the throne as still as stone. They did not roar, but their eyes were like flames as they stood noble and silent.

And from the mist appeared four living creatures with human likenesses. Their wings stretched out and touched one another. They sparkled like burnished bronze. They looked like burning coals of fire, resembling torches moving backward and forward above the throne.

Suddenly, there was a multitude of voices, thousands and thousands of them, singing in unison. Then a thunderous voice boomed with the sound of angels echoing in harmony, "You are whole."

***

Cove and the chief surgeon agreed that Heather's surgery had been successful, but they had to wait until she was out of recovery to speak to her about it and the future physical therapy that was needed to see if she would walk. Both doctors made sure to thank the anesthetist, the scrub nurse, the technical equipment handlers, and everyone else who had helped to make this procedure so successful. Cove said, "Team, after all you have done for my girl, Heather, I have supplied dinner for you in the physicians' cafeteria. Go ahead and take a long break and relax. I'll go check on Heather in recovery."

Cove stood at the edge of her bed, watching her breathing pattern, her chest rising and falling while still under the remainder of the sedative. A smile warmed his face as a vision of her dancing with him filled his mind.

Then her eyes slowly opened. Although not fully focused, she could see through the blurry vision and recognized Cove. *Perhaps it's a dream,* she thought. Perhaps if she pinched herself, she would wake up. But she didn't want to wake up. She wanted to stay in this dream of colors, angels, and wholeness.

"Cove, tell me what happened. Am I alright?" she whispered, trying to find her voice between her moans of discomfort.

Cove quickly walked to her side and held her hand. He noticed her pasty white skin from all the anesthesia, then he took out his penlight and checked her eyes. He quietly talked to her about the surgery.

"Heather, I don't want to spend too much time right now trying to explain because you really need to rest, but the good news is that all went well. Once the anesthesia has worn off, I'll explain more. You will be more alert then, but you will be in pain for a few days. You will have this IV drip of morphine, and it will ease the pain while you heal. Now sleep. No worries, just rest."

Cove felt much compassion toward her and wanted to express more, but felt it was not the time. He gave her hand a squeeze, kissed her on her cheek, and left. She felt the warmth of his kiss, like the kiss of a warrior, but could not move, for she was too dazed. She fell back to sleep.

Cove went out to the waiting room looking for her parents; he knew they were sitting there waiting for him. He ran to them, and they embraced him. He said, "Richard, Margaret, she's doing great. I'm so happy with the results."

Margaret asked with tears streaming down the side of her cheek, "Cove, we have been sitting here so anxiously. When can we see her?"

"Soon. She needs at least another hour before she can actually see you for a little while, and maybe she will be able to communicate a little. Don't worry, tomorrow will be an even better day for her. Each new day brings another day of healing to her body. I'll bring you in her room in an hour." He kissed them and walked down the hallway.

Richard and Margaret sat holding on to each other, waiting patiently.

"Richard, I hate to say this, but it feels just like when it first happened when she was only ten. My heart aches." Margaret held on to his hand very tightly.

He smoothed her hair and gave her encouragement to soothe her nerves, even though he felt the same. But he did not want to show any type of anxiety. "I know, love. But it's going to be different this time. With Cove as the surgeon and all the test results being positive, I truly believe she will walk again. Let's have faith."

***

The next several months, Heather was in intensive physical therapy. She felt she was reliving when she was ten years old, which made her more determined. Nothing would block her this time. She would walk into a fresh page of life, erasing the ones in the past of her struggles.

I worked so hard then. I was just a little girl trying to regain my life, but had to accept the diagnosis of that time: the wheelchair. This is different. I feel a strength I have never felt before. There is a kind of passion, a fire, I feel deep inside my heart, she thought as she worked with each assisted step.

She trained hard. Even though she felt some back pain, she endured. She continued to work harder with Jennifer, the physical therapist, with the locomotor training, weight-supported treadmill, and parallel bars. The therapist explained to Heather why she needed to work harder on the locomotor training.

The trainer was amazed at the strength Heather showed in her determination to walk. "Heather, you can do this. I will put you in this canvas hoist while you hold on to the side bars. I will help your legs move in a pattern. I'm trying to reteach the spinal cord and have it connected with the brain as to what it's like to walk again."

Each day, Heather would spend one hour on the locomotor training, then she would have to stand with a walker to help her spine stay straight and just take a couple of steps. Her body was sticky with perspiration that ran down the back of her neck from the hardworking muscles. She felt physically tired but thought, *I have to continue. I have to do this. I have to walk again for Cove.*

The aquatic pool brought back memories of when she had worked with her first physical therapist, Nancy, and how they would talk about Heather being a mermaid. *I'm a mermaid again, but this time my swimming fins will become my walking legs,* she thought. She remembered how cooling the water had felt and hoped all that swimming exercise would help her to walk again. This time, the water felt different. The surrounding environment felt joyful. Surprisingly, this time, her body was moving more freely.

Every muscle in my body seems stronger than it ever felt before. I feel like I can stand, but only for a moment, and then my legs give way to a shaky and weak feeling. I want to use my legs, all my limbs together. I feel my brain power working hard with my body. If I use the word believe, *I will unleash more power, so I believe.* Her thoughts continued to believe, and each day, she whispered, "I believe I am whole."

It had been three months of physical therapy when the time finally arrived where she was able to use crutches. She walked up and down the hallway and into the physical therapy room. Her therapist coached her on.

"Jennifer, this feels so different, I feel my legs, I feel my muscles in my legs. I feel a breeze on my legs! Oh Jenn, I feel my slippers on my feet, I can feel my feet touch the floor."

Heather began to shake; she bowed her head as her shoulders trembled. Her eyes welled; her tears fell to the floor as one drop fell onto her foot. Then she looked up to Jennifer.

"I felt my tears, for the first time I can feel."

Jennifer held Heather for a moment to comfort her. Jennifer shared the joy of this victory for Heather.

"Dear Heather, you are strengthening your leg muscles. Just keep your back straight. You have progressed much sooner than we all expected." She smiled as her hand smoothed over Heather's back.

It was that particular morning as she was assisted by the trainer that Cove walked in and leaned against the doorway and watched. His eyes filled with emotion as he watched her struggle against the crutches, his heart pounding out a song. He thought, *So here I stand, watching her struggle against life's disadvantages. She will win, I see it in her. I will protect her, with all that I am and ever will be.*

At that moment, Heather felt someone watching, like a shadow overlooking her. She looked up and said, "Cove! Look! I graduated from all the training equipment to this!"

With excitement, she let go of the crutches and, not realizing it, she took her first unassisted step. The physical trainer froze, then reached for her arm. Cove ran to her, then abruptly stopped.

"Heather, listen, slowly take one step toward me. Then see if you can take the next. Pace yourself. The movement has to be smooth."

She took a first step with the trainer right by her side. The trainer removed her hand to give Heather the feeling of freedom. Heather took another staggered step. Her arms still stretched out to balance herself; she took another step. They powerfully locked eyes, and it helped to keep her moving toward him. It was a silent way of saying, "Keep walking."

In eight steps, she moved unassisted to Cove. He opened his arms wide, and she walked right into them. In that moment, as they wrapped their arms around each other, they reunited their bodies and their souls. It was almost magical. She rested her head on his chest, and they cried.

***

After three months of physical therapy, Heather was released from the hospital's rehabilitation center and returned home. She was assigned a therapist to spend each day with her continuing therapy. She felt comfortable in her own apartment where she was able to retrain herself to carefully move around with each step. She thought, *I have to stay focused, I have to keep my goals, it's okay to have help while I return to full strength. This will help my progress; I still can't believe I'm walking!*

The nurse made her daily visits from early morning to late evening. She helped Heather to retrain all that she had learned at the hospital. As simple as setting her table for breakfast, lifting simple objects like a cooking pan, and to making a cup of coffee.

A social worker also made visits once a week to make sure that everything happens when it should. She would watch as Heather would attempt to use her legs to walk from one room to the other. She would log her information.

Richard and Margaret would visit Heather every day when it was time for her to take a break from the therapy. They would sit have coffee and cookies. They watched as Heather easily lifted her arm holding the cup to take a sip. Their eyes held back the emotions as they watched their daughter struggle to be well. Their hearts full of joy to see her recovery.

Jill also made sure to stop by each evening and would sleep over every other night and alternate evenings with Richard and Margaret so Heather wouldn't be alone.

Cove was there every day, in between surgeries or his day off, just to be with her, to have meals with her, never left her side. He watched as she began to walk more smoothly around the room. He was thankful that the surgery was a success. Each night before he left, he would hold her, she would embrace him, together they couldn't let go. They held soaring feelings of joy and love and the beauty of life.

Chapter 17
Precious Stone

The shadows of a painful life fell behind Heather, and she shifted into a new one. After the long days of being in so much pain ebbed, she rejoiced in the new life she had received. All the physical therapy was over. She was able to move on her own now.

The aroma of coffee coming from the kitchen gave Heather a pleasant way of waking up. She was glad she had set the timer on the coffee pot the night before. She thought, *For so long, I liked the idea of a hot cup of coffee in my own kitchen. Now I can do it.* It felt good, even unusual, to be standing up straight and tall in her kitchen, sipping her cup of coffee. She walked over to the windowsill, drinking her coffee, and as she looked out, she said, "Thank you for allowing me to live a life again, to make me strong, to give my legs back to me." With tears in her eyes, she turned her face upward to the sky.

A couple of weeks passed, and Heather was ready to meet everyone at Cove's parents' home. They were all together, her parents, Jill's parents, John, sitting in the living room of Cove's parents' home. All were waiting, excited to see for the first time Heather to actually leave her apartment and come out for dinner. But there was a secret they all knew about, a secret that was about to be revealed. Cove walked her into the house and guided her into the living room. She stood in the entrance of the living room and spread her arms out and with a wide smile.

"Here I am, looking straight at you, what do you think?"

Heather's parents ran to her, embracing her.

"My child, you are a warrior, this brings back the memory of your ballerina long legs." Margaret couldn't talk any longer, the intense moment blocked her words. Richard could just hold her as waves of tears like an ocean continued to pour out onto her hair. He couldn't let go. Jill ran over grabbed her hands.

"Heather, this is a new Heather for me. You have emerged in a brand-new world. Welcome, my sister." She couldn't reach Heather's face since her parents wouldn't lose their grip on her. So, she just held onto her hands, kissed them, and cried.

Cove gently helped them to let go and walked Heather over to his parents.

"Heather, this is a miracle. You're beautiful; to see you standing is to see your soul shining through. You're like a butterfly who has just left her cocoon. Thank God." Mary and Joseph together wrapped their arms around her, she felt warmth and comfort.

John walked over to Heather, a little shy and unable to speak at first. Then he just held her shoulders and looked straight into her eyes.

"Heather, I am so happy that you and my best friend fell in love. You have both been through so much together. I am so thankful to be a part of your lives. You're like a sister to me."

Cove then guided her to one of the sofas and sat next to her. They all talked about the surgery and the outcome. And all were thanking Cove for his part in the surgery. Then Heather noticed a sparkle on Jill's hand.

Heather held Jill's hand and inspected the diamond. "Jill, what a surprise! I am so happy that you two became engaged. We can start planning your wedding now that I can walk. I mean, I will be your maid of honor, right?"

"It was only yesterday we were walking through Central Park, taking our usual walk by the lake. We sat down and admired the scenery when he brought out this little velvet box and proposed. I tell you, John really surprised me, he never dropped a clue." Jill turned to John, glowing as he sat there liked a bird puffed up with a healthy sense of pride. They both showed a feeling of deep, abiding love that filled their hearts. With her hand holding Heather's she said.

"There is no one else who could take your place. You are my maid of honor. We will start looking at wedding halls soon, then we will decide on the bridesmaids' dress colors."

Then Heather began talking about her accident. She and Cove thought back to the time when they were both ten years old and they first met at the beach.

"Imagine, at ten, we already were in love. Just finding that seashell was the beginning of our journey."

Cove held her hand and gazed into her emerald eyes. Then they started sharing their exuberant feelings about the successful surgery.

Heather explained, "After the surgery, I thought all the physical therapy would never end. It was a reminder of the first time I had to endure it. But this was different in a way. That first moment I took steps on my own was an emotional milestone in my recovery. I will never forget! I didn't know Cove was watching me, but I felt eyes on me. When I looked up and saw Cove, just looking at his face made me want to continue walking on my own. It was magical. I couldn't take my eyes off him, and I felt power leading me to him. It's amazing how the human body can actually heal itself—that is, with the help of God and new technology." Heather stood up straight with her arms out, imitating an angel's wings. "Here I stand, having won my struggle that I never thought would end."

Her features formed into a pleased and proud smile as she stood, strong yet graceful. Everyone in the room stood and applauded.

"I have to share with you a dream I had while under anesthesia. It was so unusual. I felt like I was in Heaven. Everything I saw was what I had read in the Bible. It was like a painting of the sky of Heaven, but in a new light. Then, at the end of the dream, I heard a voice. Not just any voice, but a strong voice, which I believe was God's. He gave me a message. He said, 'You are whole.'" She smiled through happy tears while her voice cracked.

Margaret turned to her with her own tears of joy, embracing her tightly and comforting her.

"Heather, my little girl, I love you so much. I have been praying for you ever since the accident and through the surgery. I felt the good Lord tell me you would walk. When you were in the accident and the doctor was explaining all that had happened to you, I couldn't talk. I froze. All I could ask was, 'Will she walk?' He couldn't really answer me, but I knew someday you would. That dream was telling you and all of us that He is in control and that He does answer prayers."

She then let go of Heather and sat next to her, dabbing her tears away. "Heather, you walked a map of scars, from the accident and now again to another life after physical therapy. You have endured much, but you have achieved much. Look at you! You achieved your goal. You emerged victorious!"

Cove had a smile that cracked his face and an inner glow that shone outward. Then he drifted into more of his own serious thoughts.

Heather reached out for his hand. "Oh, Cove, your love for me is a gift. After all the time that passed in our lives, you found me and were determined to prove your love. And through your determination with this surgery, you have."

Then Cove's father got up from the sofa, gave a quick wink to Cove, and headed toward the dining room. He returned with a silver tray of cookies, long-stemmed crystal champagne glasses, a bottle of champagne, and a bouquet of sunflowers.

"Well, I think it's time for a little dessert and a toast to good health, don't you all agree?" Then he gave Cove a sideways glance and a big smile.

Cove looked over to his family. He took the bouquet of sunflowers and moved closer to Heather, kneeled down, and stared up to her.

"Heather, all the memories from the time we first met at the beach at only ten years old have been locked into my heart. We were arranged to be together from the beginning. I will not let go of you. Will you marry me?"

Heather loved the sunflower bouquet but didn't see the ring. She answered anyway, "Cove, yes, oh yes, my Cove."

He handed her the bouquet, which had a pink ribbon tying it together. Her fingers felt the ribbon and followed it around when she felt something at the end.

"Oh, Cove, it's a diamond!"

He carefully untied the ribbon and placed the ring on her finger.

Heather's eyes glowed with an inner light as she trembled with joy. Her hands held his tightly as she leaned forward and focused on his eyes. Then he lifted her up and held her. There was no music, just the sounds of love and joy that made them dance. They swayed slowly to the silent music with the pressure of his warm hand on her back guiding her along the floor. Their eyes locked, never blinking.

"You see, Heather, your dream has come true. You will dance again—with me, at our wedding."

***

The following week, Heather was energetically getting ready for work when she noticed her wheelchair in the living room. She walked over, touched the top of the soft, woven chair, then ran her finger across and down to the steel armrest. Then she folded it up and rolled it to her closet. There was more than enough room to store it there.

Once it was in place, she felt disconnected, like something had been taken from her. She was happy to be able to walk, stand, and bend. But there was another feeling she hadn't expected. It was like saying goodbye to a best friend. She knelt down and placed one hand on the armrest. She felt a tear run down from her eye.

"Well, Mr. Steel, for over twenty years, you have been a very important part of my life. You have taken care of me and have been through all my trials and joys. I will never use you again, but I will never give you away. You will always be a reminder to me of our travels through life together."

Her heart beat in a steady rhythm as she let out a soft sigh. It signaled the end of all their efforts together and the beginning of gladness in leaving the old path behind. As if taking her last breath, she slowly closed the door, her eyes still peeking at the edge. There was a soft gleam, then a sudden, small flash of light that shone from the silver steel. It was resolved.

***

It was her first day back at work. As she was just about ready to leave, she thought, *Today will be different. I can walk to the elevator. I can walk with Jill to work.*

"Good morning, Mr. Bates! How are you today?" Her eyes were different this time, brighter, to go along with her confident speech and a wide smile.

"Good morning, young lady. It's good to see you around and about again after your surgery. I'm glad you're doing so well. I was worried about you and thought of you often." Mr. Bates almost had tears of joy in his eyes. "Okay, here's your stop." He gave her a loving smile as she walked out.

"Thanks, Mr. Bates." She returned the smile as if she had won the lottery.

Mr. Santos was waiting at the front entrance for her. As usual, he tipped his hat. "Buenos días, Miss Heather. So good to see you again. You look very well. I am happy." There was a softness to his appearance and a little shyness as he glanced downward for a moment.

"Oh, Mr. Santos, it is so very good to be back. Buenos días and adios." She gave him a soft laugh and went out the door.

She was able to meet Jill for their usual commute to the lab together. She looked forward to her time with Jill like any other day, but this day was different. There wasn't a car with driving gadgets to use. She would actually walk to work with her strong legs this time. She had never dreamed this would happen. Her heart leaped with the confidence of a prima ballerina. She felt like a supermodel walking down the runway with long, streamlined legs as she walked to the lab with Jill.

"Wow, Heather, this is awesome walking with you! We are eye to eye. Same height!"

Then Jill stopped and just stared at Heather, her emotions caught in her throat. She grabbed Heather and sobbed with joy. Heather didn't care that they stopped in the traffic of city workers, she just held on to Jill.

"Dear Jill, my forever sister and friend."

They finally arrived at their job, but the entrance door was locked. Heather thought, *This is unusual. Dr. Harris is always the first one in and keeps the doors unlocked.*

"Jill, why is this door locked? Where is Dr. Harris?" Heather fumbled for the keys at the bottom of her bag.

"I have no idea. I hope everything is okay in there. Here, I have the key." Jill slowly unlocked the door.

Just as they walked into the entrance room, there was a loud burst of voices yelling, "Surprise! Congratulations!"

Every doctor, every technician, and every pathologist were there. Hung above was a sign saying CONGRATULATIONS ON YOUR WEDDING. Balloons and streamers of every color dangled from the ceiling and down the walls. Every desk was decorated with flowers and candles, and in the center of the room was a large table that held a cake with the words *Love Eternal for Robert and Heather*.

For a moment, Heather stood in shock. Her body couldn't move. Even her legs shook. The shock wore off, her breath became steady and she could taste the salted tears. Jill and everyone gathered around her, hugging her and wishing the best for her. Heather's eyes became larger than life as she noticed all the gifts on a separate table. There was another table set off to the side decorated with a white tablecloth and candles that featured an arrangement of sandwiches, fruit bowls, and salads of all types.

Just then, the door opened again. Cove entered the room with a happy bounce, smiling and laughing a childish laugh despite his age.

"Surprise, Heather! I was so afraid I would let this secret out."

He wrapped his arms around her, and she intensely squeezed him back.

"You knew all along? I can't believe this. This is all so generous, so loving. I'm at a loss for words."

"Well, now, let's get this party started. Sit here, Heather. We'll start opening just a few gifts, then we'll stop and eat!" Jill, acting as if she were being tickled, ran to get the first gift.

No one worked that day. It was a day of celebration for everyone as they watched Heather—their cytotechnologist, their dear friend who had been healed.

Chapter 18
The Wedding

Time moved quickly for Cove and Heather; in just four months all the preparation was complete. Margaret and Richard worked together with Joseph and Mary in all the arrangements. Even Jill's parents, Jeff and Jillian, joined in the excitement of helping in the wedding. John pitched in when needed to climb up high, attaching the lights onto the beams of the catering hall. Everything was put in place. The wedding would be held in a natural woodland setting. Heather and Cove agreed that they wanted to honor God in His creation as a thank-you for all the healing He had brought to their lives. It was a beautiful, early-summer morning. Heather and Margaret sat in the bridal suite of the chapel preparing for the wedding. Jill, being her maid of honor, was in the other room fixing her gown and her hair while loudly singing like a songbird, smooth and clear.

"Heather, darling, I have been saving this genuine pearl necklace for you since you were born. I knew someday you would wear it on your wedding day. Even through the tragic time after the accident, I held on to hope and faith, and I really believed that someday I would hand this to you. It was your great-grandmother's. She wore it on her wedding day. So did Grandma, and so did I."

Margaret gently placed the pearls around her daughter's neck. A glow appeared to her skin as it rested around her neck, like a gift from Heaven.

"Mom, it's beautiful. You know, it reminds me of when Cove and I opened that shell. I actually thought there would be a pearl inside. And then he laughed when I said that. Imagine, we were only ten then. Who would have thought we would be married? And now I have the pearl—a whole string of them!" She could feel the smoothness touching her skin as she tenderly touched the lustrous gems.

Suddenly, the door burst open as Jill made a grand entrance into the room, full of vigor. "Okay, Heather, Margaret; here I am. Like the color of my gown? And look at my engagement ring. It just glitters against the color of my dress!"

Heather said, "Oh, Jill, you are quite the exuberant one, and yes, your ring is truly beautiful. We will be working on your wedding arrangements next. This is all so wonderful for both of us. Well, I'm ready. Come on, Mom, Jill; let's get Dad."

The three linked arms as they walked down the hallway to the top of the steps. Heather and Margaret waited for a sign to start walking down the staircase. Jill ran ahead and waited for Richard so she could wave to the small ensemble to begin Heather's walk to the altar.

In another private room downstairs, Richard and Cove were just finishing up putting on their tuxedos.

"Here, son, let me straighten your bow tie. You don't want to be standing there with a twisted tie, do you?"

Richard said with a nervous laugh, trying to cover the emotions he felt flooding in.

"Richard, I love your daughter so much, and you and Margaret so quickly included me into your family, it just came together so naturally. Right now, I feel this is one of the greatest moments life can bring to me." They shook hands, and then Richard just pulled Cove into his arms.

"Cove, this is a great moment for you and my daughter, but the greatest moment was when she began to walk. We don't understand why all these strange things happened— you two meeting as children, the accident—but one thing is for sure: it was our faith in God that placed all things together for good. I thank God for healing my daughter, and I thank God for giving you the gift of surgical hands." And with a loving pat on Cove's shoulder, they took one last look in the mirror. They were ready.

The time had arrived. Both nervous, they stepped out of the room like stepping onto a stage.

Jill saw them from the top of the staircase and waved for Cove to go ahead to the altar where the minister and Cove's best man, John, were waiting.

On this day, the sunlight was at its most brilliant, reflecting through each of the surrounding trees, giving a warm and steady feeling of pure joy to everyone seated. The gentle sound of music filled the air, its sound rushing in and out like the waves of the ocean, moving among the humming of chatter from the guests waiting in anticipation of Heather and Cove's union.

And it began. Margaret was first to walk down the white aisle runner, escorted by one of the ushers. At the end of each pew was an arrangement of scented lavender accented with white baby's breath, and in the middle was one sunflower. Jill followed, wearing an earth-tone dress of rust, holding her bouquet of baby's breath, red berries, and sunflowers. Cove and John anxiously waited at the altar. John smiled a loving smile at Jill as he watched her walk toward them. He thought, *How beautiful she is, and she will be the next bride, my bride.*

Cove kept his eyes ahead, waiting for his bride, when at that moment he saw her arm in arm with Richard. Heather and her dad walked under the trees that formed an arch in the back of the catering hall. She was in the spotlight, and her face shone like a bright light. Her gown—a white, beaded lace dress that flowed with each step—was as pure as her love. The veil just below her chin couldn't hide her flushed cheeks, and the pearl necklace shimmered in the sunlight. She held tightly with one hand her bouquet, which was filled with burnt-orange roses, purple orchids, baby's breath, and one sunflower in the center. Richard held her arm tightly, not just to steady her but to keep himself focused. He moved slowly, hoping no one would notice the one tear running down his cheek.

The long walk ended. Richard turned to Heather and lifted her veil. She looked up at him with her big, emerald-green eyes and squeezed his hand. He gave her a loving kiss on her forehead and gave her hand to Cove.

Cove took her hands and held them in his as he looked directly into her. As if there were no one around, he spoke his vows to her.

"You were my soul mate from the day we met at the beach; even at ten we were united. To think a little seashell, like the form of a love letter that we never lost, both of us

218

tucked it away until it brought us back together again. I fell in love with you the day we met, and I fell in love with you more deeply the second time, decades later. You are now who you were born to become."

Cove's heart beat faster, and his body trembled with excitement.

Heather's gaze never left his eyes; her face glowed like the moon lit up at night.

"The man that stands before me is the first real love I've ever experienced. You represent the finest of a love letter with words of true emotions locked in my heart. I could wrap myself up in your words, for you are my love poem. With one touch, one shell that summer day on the beach, you entered my soul."

Her lip trembled, and a tear ran down her face.

They placed their wedding bands on each other's finger, bands curved as three strands symbolized their souls knitted together with God. Then their first kiss as husband and wife was like their souls whispered, *together now you are one*.

There was a rush of emotion as John watched his best friend marry the girl of his dreams, then he looked at Jill and thought of their future wedding and the excitement of being her husband and Jill being his wife.

All the parents felt the same watching Cove and Heather taking the vows. It was an emotional journey, feeling hope and tender affection for them both.

The love of their marriage was simple and pure, the bond of a blessed couple. As they held each other while taking their vows, it was like the beauty of their love was captured in a photograph.

The reception room buzzed with excitement and laughter as children ran between tables. The hall was draped with tiny softly glowing lights intertwined with baby-pink roses. The wedding cake towered high with layers that the mother of the bride and the mother of the groom had combined. Each layer was a personal family favorite, giving a traditional, homemade touch. At the sides of each layer was a fresh, dusky-red rose, and sugar seashells studded each layer of the cake as remembrance of their meeting and their connection. Just as their love was easy and sweet, so was their wedding cake.

The illuminated dance floor was like dancing on the northern lights. As multiple colors shone through the wood floor, Cove took her in his arms for their first dance. The music played over the dance floor, and they moved smoothly, as if it had fused with their bodies. Heather's legs felt strong and graceful as she took each step to the beat, gliding and swaying to the sound. Cove kept his hand on the small of her back, holding her tightly as they swirled to the music. They had practiced the dance before to make sure she felt strong enough, but this was her first actual dance in public. Her legs felt the freedom of the movement like a new breath of nourishment for her soul as she could now dance upon the polished wood floor. The music drifted out of the reception room like a vibrating pulse. The night was alive with joy and fulfilled dreams.

It was time for the bride to dance with her father. Heather had chosen the Ben E. King song "Stand by Me," but before they began their dance, she made an announcement.

"Dad, I dedicate this song to you because I've always been your little girl. You taught me to ride my bicycle, and you taught me that I can do anything in any situation, even in my wheelchair. You and Mom have encouraged me to be strong and never be afraid, never to fear the darkness, no matter what happens. You both always would stand by me." Then she recited the first verse:

"When the night has come
And the land is dark
And the moon is the only light we'll see
No, I won't be afraid
Oh, I won't be afraid
Just as long as you stand, stand by me."

Her tribute to her father was a sweet moment as they danced across the shiny floor. She rested her head on his shoulder as they moved slowly, like gliding across water. With wet eyes, he whispered, "I feel like when you were little, and we would dance in the living room. You would keep your feet on top of mine, and we would move to the music."

"Yes, Dad," she said in a low voice.

Then she waved to Cove. He knew what was next. He took Margaret by the arm and brought her to the dance floor. Heather held her mother and father, and the three of them danced to the song dedicated to her parents.

Heather said, "Mom, did you think I would forget you? We are a family. Thank you for all your support. I know how much you wanted to be a ballet dancer, and you wished the same for me. We can both take off our thoughts of ballet slippers. We hold the wisdom of dance in our hearts."

"Heather, we are no longer dancers, but we dance for the Lord in our hearts, for He set the stage of life. He is the choreographer!"

The music changed to an upbeat rhythm. Then John took hold of Jill and brought her to the dance floor. They dance and spun while the lights twinkled with every beat. John turned her in delicate circles while her dress billowed out. Then the music changed to a slower style, and more people entered the dance floor.

As he held her in his arms, moving to the slow sound of the music, he whispered, "Jill, we can plan our wedding now. Tomorrow, we set a date." He nuzzled his nose into her hair. "Cove will be my best man, of course, and I'm sure Heather will be your maid of honor. Oh wait, she's married now, so she'll be your matron of honor."

Jill gazed in awe as he spoke to her, thinking how much she loved and admired him, she lingered on each word as he spoke.

"You know our love is strong. We will make a great life together. If you think of it, if Cove hadn't met Heather, I wouldn't have met you." Then he kissed her. It was a heavenly kiss, like a kiss in the rain.

The night ended with sweet congratulations, best wishes, and goodbyes.

Richard said to Heather, "You're married now, but you're still my sweet little girl. I meant to tell you, your mom and I tried to watch that *Father of the Bride* movie the other night, and we had to turn it off. But today, I feel so

proud of the both of you. Cove, we are truly a family."
Richard hugged them both, and Margaret joined in. Then
they left.

Cove's parents came rushing over to give them both
hugs and kisses.

Mary said, "My kids, I'm so happy for you. This was a
wonderful wedding. We will all get together when you
return and have a private family dinner."

Mary held them both. Then she took her son's hands.
"Cove, you have worked so hard over the years with your
studies and travels to other countries. I'm so happy that you
returned to us, but especially to Heather. She is more than a
daughter-in-law. She is our daughter."

Cove's dad gave Heather a father's kiss. "Young lady,
you are now our daughter. I couldn't be happier. I look
forward to many holidays being spent together. God bless
you, my child."

Finally, when everyone had left, Cove lifted her hands
to his chest and told her he had a surprise for her.

Heather's eyes lit up. "Cove, what could be more
amazing than what I just experienced?" She giggled.

"Well, I think it's our honeymoon. I can't tell you; I
have to surprise you. It's something you've always wanted.
Come on, let's go." Cove was now eager to reveal this
secret.

The car ride was not long. Within an hour, they had
reached their destination. She knew by the exits where they
were going. Her heartbeat pulsed through her body with
excitement. Then they parked. Still in her wedding dress, he
picked her up and carried her to the beach, their beach. He
inspired her. His eyes said what words could never say.

"Heather, this is where we met. This is our home. Here is where we will resume where we left off so long ago. Let's just sit here."

"But Cove, my wedding dress, it's picking up all the sand." Then she saw how serious his eyes and face became, so she sat, and he wrapped his arms around her.

"Heather, just sit and watch the stars that are like guardians of the galaxy."

She tilted her head back onto his shoulder, and they gazed upward into the black curtain that draped over the sky. The silver glow of the moon shone onto the ocean like a path upon the waters.

"You're right, Cove. I was never able to come back to the beach and enjoy by actually sitting and feeling the sand again under my feet. I was never able to sit here in the moonlight and see these beautiful, blinking fairy lights in the night sky like little fireflies that made me want to reach out and catch them." She lifted her hand, imitating catching one.

"In ancient times, the sky and the stars were used for navigation. Years after our first meeting, it looks like we were guided right back to where we first met." He held her hand and felt the rings on her finger, then lifted her hand and gave it a kiss.

They sat for a while reminiscing about their childhood meeting and all the memories that it awakened. She remembered how they had run to the shore and collected buckets of shells, and then she remembered the seashell and how he had given her half, as if it were a ring of friendship. They could feel the ocean breeze whispering to them and leaving salty kisses on their cheeks. They kissed in a soft and comforting way that words could never be. She could feel his beating heart against her chest.

It was time to leave. But Cove said, "My Heather, I have one more surprise. Let's take a walk."

They brushed off the sand and walked over the small bridge to the street.

"Cove, I remember this little bridge and this particular stone street. I think I know where we are going. Memories are flooding my mind."

They came to a small, white cottage just two blocks from the beach.

Heather felt the muscles of her chin tremble like the little girl she was once.

"It's my summer home!"

They entered the front door and walked into a dimly lit room filled with the fragrance of hydrangea and lavender. The small coffee table held a bottle of champagne and two crystal long-stemmed glasses. And there right alongside of the glasses was the seashell, as if it had just been found again, semitranslucent white and whole. She picked it up, feeling its ridged edges as she did when she was ten years old.

"Cove, you attached the shells together. It's closed as if it's one shell again. It's beautiful."

"Heather, it's a symbol of our lives. This is where we met, and this is where we begin our new life. It will be our summer home where we will bring our children here every summer just like your parents did. We will retire here. We will live all our years here through all our summers. You deserve all this and more, Mrs. Ferris."

She sobbed with joy into his chest as he silently held her, rocking her slowly. She closed her eyes to the lullaby of the ocean, breathing in its misty scent. They reached for the shell and smiled. Then, with every kiss, the passion rose with their pounding heartbeats like the deep current of the ocean waves. The tiny shell with its magical imprint rested in the hands that found it.